THE GODS ABOVE

Alex McGilvery

The God's Above

Alex McGilvery

Cover Illustration

Alex McGilvery

ZOMBIE WALK

Pranthi shuffled slightly faster than the horde of zombies following her. They were gaining on her. Time to do something before they caught up. She turned and snapped a couple of pictures. The zombie walkers were a decent crop this year. One of the men had a hole through his chest. Pranthi could see another shambling zombie behind him. She took some more pictures, working hard to stay ahead of the mob, but finally gave up.

The horde lurched past her, ignoring her and her camera just as the organizers asked them every year.

"How about lunch?" a zombie near the back mumbled past ketchup, wax and cheap fake teeth. There was one every year. Pranthi shook her head and shot a few more of the stragglers. The ones at the back didn't have the make-up that would win them a cash prize, but they had the best zombie walk. Most of the crowd were too eager to get to the finish and tuck into the free donuts and coffee to shamble properly. Even in still shots the shamblers' slumped postures looked good. If someone combined make-up and acting effort, it would make for some brilliant photos.

She'd photographed at least five zombie walks now. At first they were a fringe thing, but in the past couple of years they'd become big business. Tens of thousands of dollars and mountains of tins of food were raised by these walks. The organizers handed out cards and brochures offering to set up any kind of event desired. Pranthi's photographs were icing on the cake, as more than enough people bought pictures of themselves as the living dead to compensate for the fee she charged for the day. A few more shots from the back and Pranthi headed through the crowd to a coffee shop at the side of the street.

The leg braces she wore over her skinny jeans kept people at arm's length. She didn't mind. Talking was the last thing on her mind. What she wanted came in a tall cup with foam and a sprinkle of cinnamon on top. She snapped some pictures while waiting in line. A couple of walkers clearly thought the quality of the free coffee was suspect. The barista was a good sport and gave her a wide grin even as she didn't look right at the camera.

"Hi, Pranthi," Pat said as she pushed the coffee

across the counter. Her name tag read 'Tina'. Pat didn't like people knowing her name. Everyone had their hang-ups. The only concession Pranthi made to her legs was to let Pat carry the coffee to a table for her. She sat in the corner and rubbed her thighs through the gaps in the steel. The braces let her walk, but they hurt like hell.

The latte revived her and the ache receded enough for her to pull out her tablet and load the pictures from her cameras. She had a hard time remembering all the fussing she had to do last year to check her shots. She put out offerings regularly, in thanks, for whoever mated Wi-Fi with cameras and made her life easier.

They weren't bad, not her best work, but good enough for the organizers. They wanted zombie shots for their publicity work, not art shots. They paid enough to keep Pranthi in lattes and that was all that mattered.

"Hey, there." A young woman sat down across from Pranthi and dropped a bag with a clunk on the floor. "You were shooting zombies," she smiled and sipped at her drink. To Pranthi's amazement, she didn't immediately try to crane her neck to see what was on the tablet. Too many people thought what she had on the tablet was public property. She looked closer at the woman. Blood red stains on her fingers suggested she'd worked on at least one zombie's make-up. The bag probably held more gear to repair whatever damage the walk did before the judges chose their favourite.

"That would be me," Pranthi waved at the cameras. The other woman laughed and Pranthi's stomach filled with butterflies. Conversations made her nervous.

The woman's eyes were the blue of the Indian Ocean, not the mud of her own. Pranthi never knew how to talk to people, especially not beautiful people who should be ignoring her, not smiling like they were old friends. Instead of talking she flipped over the tablet and watched the woman scroll through the pictures. Technically, it was a breach of her agreement with the organizers, but what they didn't know wouldn't hurt them. It wasn't as if Pranthi was going sell photos to this woman.

"This one is brilliant," the woman held up a shot Pranthi knew the organizers would hate because they couldn't sell it to the zombies. It showed a blurred face in the foreground with a zombie in the mid-ground with a hand outstretched. The camera angle made it look like the hand was on the first person's shoulder. The background faded to a riot of colour. Because this blue-eyed woman liked it, Pranthi loved it too. The woman flipped through a few other shots before she snorted and showed Pranthi the shot of the man with the hole through him.

"This one," the woman made a face and Pranthi laughed. "I designed and built that for him. It took weeks to get the programming right. Anyone can tape two tablets and sync the cameras. I set it up so occasionally blood spurts across the wound. How does he thank me? He asks me to make up his new girlfriend so they can enter the pairs contest."

"And you did?" Pranthi asked.

"Yeah, I did." The woman sipped at her drink and went back to aimlessly flipping through pictures, but now she barely looked at them. "Couldn't make them more like zombies without killing them."

"Some people are hard to refuse," Pranthi said to break the silence. It was that or ask for her tablet back.

"Spoken like the voice of experience."

"Yeah, except with me it is family," Pranthi sipped her latte and tried to stop her tongue. Not bloody likely. "I live on my own so it is harder for them to try to find me a husband."

"I'm guessing the idea of a husband doesn't thrill you." Her words came out dry and bitter as she slid the tablet back to Pranthi.

"I'm already married to my camera."

The woman put her hand on Pranthi's and warmth travelled up her arm. Touch was scarier than conversation. She froze, but the woman didn't notice.

"Ironic that the modern idea of zombies has nothing to do with science."

"There are zombies in science?"

"Sure," to Pranthi's relief she leaned back again, freeing Pranthi's arm. "A fungus takes over one species of ant and forces it to climb high in the foliage where a certain species of bird eats it and spreads the spores through the forest. A parasite takes over a beetle and makes it go to where the eggs in the beetle are more likely to hatch. Nature is cruel."

"Nasty, for sure," Pranthi said.

"Stay. Look at your pictures, and by the time you get them handed in, it will be all over."

"What?" Pranthi pulled her hand away. "What did you do?" A different heat filled her as she imagined bombs or guns or other horrors shown on the news nightly.

The woman laughed and sipped her drink.

"Nothing so final as you're imagining from the look on your face," she shrugged and looked away, but not before a tear rolled down her cheek. "I worked so hard for him, and he runs after that bimbo. Biology. Nothing I can do about that. So I gave him a parting gift. Let him experience what being a zombie might feel like."

"How can you make him feel like the undead?"

"No," the woman frowned and drank the last of her coffee. "Not undead. Like an ant who will seek the heights and the sun to be consumed. It won't last."

Pranthi's phone rang, breaking the moment.

"What the heck are you doing?" Kevin, the lead organizer, yelled at Pranthi over the phone. "I need you here to shoot the winners."

"My legs got tired," Pranthi said, "I stopped to give them a break."

"Yeah, you have my sympathy, but your contract says you'll shoot the winners and we'll be choosing them in just a few minutes. Where are you? I'll come get you."

"I'm at a coffee shop about halfway through the route." Pranthi slugged back the last of her latte. "I'll wait for you outside."

"If you must go," the woman leaned over and kissed Pranthi on the lips. "Just go ahead and forget me." She crushed her empty cup and stuffed it in her bag before walking out of the coffee shop.

The brief kiss emptied Pranthi's mind and she had no idea how long she would have sat there with her fingers on her lips if her cell phone hadn't rung again. "I'm out front," Kevin said. "Where are you?"

Pranthi swept her tablet into her bag and gave the table a quick glance for loose gear. She hobbled out to the street where Kevin's black Prius blocked traffic. The honking behind him didn't make him move until she'd crawled into the car and closed the door.

"You'll be able to do the rest of the day?" he asked as she buckled her seatbelt. The switch from angry yelling on the phone to concern made her head spin.

"Sure," Pranthi said, "sorry to be a trouble."

"No trouble," Kevin said, "but you know business is business."

"I have shots of everyone on the walk," Pranthi said. "If not individual, at least in groups."

"We may get a stationary booth set up next year for people to get staged shots," Kevin pulled into the field where zombies milled about eating donuts instead of brains. "Then you can concentrate on those art shots you keep trying to sell us."

Pranthi climbed out of the car and checked her

gear. The last thing she needed was Kevin returning anything to her apartment. Nice enough the couple of times a year she worked for him, but she didn't need any friends. They got in the way.

Kevin ran to the podium where Amelia, his business partner, waited with a handful of envelopes.

"Okay, then," Kevin said into the PA system, "let's get to the part you've been waiting so patiently for." He pulled the list from his pocket as screaming started off to the side. Pranthi lifted her camera automatically and got a picture of a growing crowd of zombies running toward her.

"Calm down," Kevin said, "the sooner we have quiet, the sooner I can hand out money."

The noise grew louder as the people ran past the stage and past Pranthi. She framed a shot of the hole-right-through-him zombie lurching after people, red dripping from his mouth a brighter color than the stains on his shirt. A blonde zombie lay on the ground behind him with more of that brighter red on her throat and chest.

Red shifted into blood in Pranthi's mind as the spurts from the blonde's neck stopped. By the time she framed the man in her viewfinder, he'd caught a slower member of the fleeing crowd and was gnawing on her neck. Blood flowed and her shrill cries faded until she stopped trying to push the man away. He dropped her to the ground and shuffled on.

Pranthi increased the shutter speed to compensate for her shaking hands. No one stood between Pranthi and the man who had now killed two people, and even with him doing a top-notch zombie walk now, he still moved faster than Pranthi's exhausted legs could. Since she wasn't going to be able to outrun him, she kept shooting pictures as he got closer. Something to distract her from her imminent death.

Blood dripped from his mouth and his eyes had a strange white film on them. Arms and legs moved spastically, as if he were fighting against himself as he walked. His tongue hung out as he got close enough for her to switch to her wide-angle lens. That's when Kevin hit the man from behind with a mic stand. The zombie fell to the ground, twitched once and then lay still.

AFTERMATH

"I don't suppose you'd sell me the card in your camera for five grand?" Kevin asked as he came up to Pranthi, still carrying the mic stand. Blood spattered his shirt, but he spoke no differently than he ever had.

"These shots are worth twice that," Pranthi said.

"Did you at least get a picture of me dinging that clown?" Kevin dropped the mic stand and turned away to vomit on the grass. Pranthi took pictures of the downed zombie walker so she didn't need to watch.

Kevin wiped his face with his sleeve before noticing the red covering it. He threw up some more before pulling out his cell phone and dialing 911.

***

Most of the crowd had vanished before the police arrived.

"We need the card from your camera, ma'am," the sergeant said to her after she'd given her statement for the third time. Her legs ached, her head ached. Something important nibbled at the back of her mind, but she didn't have the energy to pursue it.

"You have a warrant?" Pranthi clutched at her camera until her fingers ached. "These pictures are my livelihood. You can get a warrant and have a fight on your hands, or you let me copy the pictures and give you the copy."

"How long do you need?" the sergeant asked.

"Leave me alone for two minutes and I'll have them for you." The cop nodded and stood over her while she copied the pictures from her cards onto a USB drive. "Don't be releasing any of these without my permission." Pranthi handed him the drive and took the receipt he gave her.

"That's usually my line." The sergeant handed her a card. "If you need to talk to anyone about this experience these people are good. Free, too."

Pranthi put the card in her camera bag and packed up her gear. She gave him one of her cards.

"The files on the USB are in RAW format," she said. "If your people have trouble accessing them, give me call."

"Thanks," the sergeant said, "but we should be good."

She waved at him and walked a little ways outside the crime scene tape before pulling out her phone.

"Denise," she said when the Journal's photo editor picked up, "I have some pictures you'll want to buy from me."

"I have last year's shots from the Zombie Walk," Denise said, "why should I pay you for more?"

"You don't have pictures of a guy going off his head and chewing out the throat of a couple of women."

"Ugh," Denise said, "I need something I can print."

"I have shots you can use," Pranthi said, "or I could call the Sun."

"Zombies are more their style," Denise said. "Matt's supposed to be there, catch a ride with him and we'll talk."

Pranthi found a seat and waited. A big man with a cheap camera on a strap around his neck walked up and sat beside her.

"You're Matt?" Pranthi asked.

"I was on the other side of the park when it went down." He rolled his head a couple of times making cracking sounds, then nodded. "Some girl had her dog done up as a zombie dog."

"I'll tell you about it on the way to the paper," Pranthi said.

"Sounds like a deal," Matt said. He groaned as

he stood up. "At least the dog was cute."

Pranthi let him carry her gear bag to his car. Matt let her climb in before closing the door and driving off.

"So, what happened?" he asked her as he cut off a garbage truck.

"I'm not sure." Pranthi hung on to her camera bag with one hand, the handle over the door with the other. She slid the bag to the floor. If the airbags went off, she didn't want any of her gear getting damaged.

"Come on," Matt said, "it isn't like they're going to let me actually write an important story. You said you'd fill me in."

"One of the zombies went nuts." Pranthi's hand tightened on the handle. Partly from the memory of that blank stare and partly from Matt accelerating through a yellow light. "He chewed through the throats of two women and would have got me, too, if Kevin hadn't hit him with a mic stand."

"Chewed through their necks?" Gulping sounds came from the other seat. Pranthi took her eyes from the road long enough to see that Matt had turned even whiter and had beads of sweat hanging from his forehead.

"If you are going to be sick," Pranthi said, "you

should pull over."

Matt took a deep breath, then a second.

"No," he said, "I'm good." He pulled up in front of the Journal building and parked by a fire hydrant. "I'll text Denise we're here."

Pranthi climbed out of the car and headed toward the doors of the modern glass and steel building. Matt ran briefly to catch up to her. He tried to take her gear bag again, but she shook her head and clutched it tighter.

Denise met Matt and Pranthi at the door of the Journal. Her black hair was the exact shade of the suit she wore. Her bright red lips were the only colour on her.

"I heard the bulletin on the radio. Please tell me you have permission to use these pictures of the attack." She stood in the doorway forcing Pranthi to stand on the sidewalk.

"Matt has some very cute pictures of a dog made up to be a zombie," Pranthi gave her brightest smile. The sound of Denise's teeth grinding made her grin wider, but it wasn't getting her paid. "Look, do you want to stand out here on the sidewalk and look at them, or can we find a desk? I know you have all kinds of time before the night edition comes out, but I hear a hot bath calling my name."

"Don't be sarcastic with me," Denise stepped

back from the door and let them in. It clicked shut behind them. Pranthi had a brief vision of them staring through the glass at masses of attacking zombies.

"I'm not being sarcastic," Pranthi said, "I've been on my feet all day and I need that bath."

The grinding started again as Denise led them to her office. Pranthi sat on the chair and heaved a sigh.

"You have no idea how good that feels."

"What happened to your legs?" Matt asked.

"My mother arranged to have my legs run over by a truck," Pranthi said. "She wanted me to be a more effective beggar. My sister brought me here from India, but there wasn't much they could do aside from clapping torture devices on my legs and pronouncing me cured. I'm neither married nor a beggar, and so remain a disappointment to both sister and mother."

"Can we just look at the pictures?" Denise tapped the desk between each word. Pranthi pulled her tablet out of her bag and handed it to Denise.

"Just swipe through until you see what you want. Then we'll talk price."

"I'll give you a thousand without even looking at them."

"I turned down an offer of five thousand to not

show them."

"The police cleared these?"

"No one said not to sell the shots." She smacked her head, "No, I'm wrong. I told them not to."

"I can't give you five, even if you caught the guy in the act of killing the girl."

Pranthi took the tablet back and swiped through to a series of shots, then handed it back to Denise.

She looked at the pictures and turned green. "Sorry," Denise said as she ran out of the room.

"Hope she makes it to the washroom," Pranthi said. Matt reached for the tablet but Pranthi rapped his knuckles. "Show me your dog pictures."

Matt pulled up his camera and scanned through endless pictures before handing the camera to Pranthi.

"Not too shabby," Pranthi said. "You got down to the dog's level and caught that drool coming out of his mouth. The girl looks ridiculous, but the shot's about the dog not her. Hope you aren't looking for a hot date if this gets published."

"She had a very, not-dead, boyfriend tapping his toes and talking about riding his Harley after the walk. He looked more like a scooter guy, but I make it a policy not to date girls with baggage, especially wannabe biker type baggage." He looked over at Pranthi and gave what Pranthi guessed was supposed to be a winning smile.

"Baggage, Matt," Pranthi said. She slapped her legs. "Lots of baggage."

Denise came back into the room and sat down. She picked up the tablet and scrolled through the shots.

"I can go three," Denise said. "We get everything from the walk, copyright reverts to you at the end of the week."

Pranthi looked up at the ceiling, she'd be able to sell them again to a monthly rag for an in-depth story. Someone would want to do one.

"Four and a half," Pranthi said, "and I shop them around now so they can print them before it's old news."

"Four," Denise glared at her. "Don't care when you sell them, as long as they don't print before the end of the week."

"Good enough," Pranthi said. "You want them raw or processed?"

"I'll pay whatever your usual rate for post is, if you can do it here and now. You have half an hour until I need the pictures to mock up the front page."

"Give me the sizes and I'll do them."

"I thought you wanted a bath," Denise said.

"My processing fee is a hundred bucks an hour," Pranthi said. "That will pay for the taxi." She took the tablet back from Denise. "Which ones do you want?"

She slipped the chosen shots into a folder and started working on them. Fingers flying across the screen, she bumped clarity and saturation. Newsprint ruined pictures but she'd do what she could.

"Look at Matt's picture of the cute dog, you can use it for the family section," Pranthi said without looking up from her work. Matt gave her a look of gratitude and another lopsided smile.

"Baggage, Matt," Pranthi said, her fingers still dancing over the tablet. "Not just carry-on either. Full set, hard sided. The kind that give baggage handlers hernias."

Matt laughed and showed Denise his shots.

Twenty-nine minutes later, Pranthi walked out the door with fifty dollars in cash and a signed contract for another four thousand dollars.

IT ISN'T A VIRUS

She flagged down a taxi and gave him her address. Twenty minutes of stop and go traffic later, the cab dropped her at her apartment. The meter said forty dollars, so she gave him the fifty and a smile.

As soon as she turned away, she let the smile drop. Her gear weighed her down as she hobbled to the door.

Frank, the concierge, opened the door for her.

"I've hit the call button for the elevator," he said. "You can sit in my chair to wait."

"Thanks," Pranthi said, "but if I sit down, you'll have to wheel me into my apartment."

The elevator doors opened and she walked in. Ten floors up, she staggered out into the hall and down to her room. She had her key out, so it only took seconds for her to get through the door and collapse into her wheelchair. The leg braces fell to the floor with a thump and she shuddered at the combination of both freedom and weakness.

The apartment had been set up for the wheelchair by a previous tenant, so after she hung up the braces and put her gear on the table, she rolled straight into the bathroom to run her bath. By the time she'd wriggled out of her clothes, the water filled the tub and steam fogged the mirror.

Pranthi rolled herself into the water and half sighed, half shrieked. She rubbed her legs to ease the cramps and get the blood flowing properly. The network of dark scars on her olive skin looked like a child had scribbled on her legs with a marker.

No child made those marks. Karma did that. Pranthi had stopped wondering what horrible thing some past version of her soul had done. It didn't change the facts.

The phone rang, as soon as Pranthi climbed out of the bath and wrapped up in a robe to sit in her wheelchair.

"Hi," she said. "One of these days, I'm going to find the camera in my bathroom."

"Don't be ridiculous," her sister said. "I saw the news. Please tell me you weren't at that awful walk. Someone died."

"I made four grand on my photos," Pranthi said, "and I'll make more in a week or two. I'll give you some to send over home."

"You don't need the money," her sister said. "You could live with us and not have to put yourself in danger over silly photographs."

"That is the very reason I live in my own place." Pranthi wheeled to the kitchen and slapped some rice and curry on a plate and shoved it into the microwave. "Those photographs are the only thing making life worth living."

"I just don't want you getting hurt. A good man will bring meaning to your life."

"I don't need a man to take care of me."

An image, like a photograph, flashed in her mind of the deranged man tearing out that girl's throat, and another of Kevin after he killed the zombie killed Pranthi's appetite.

"The truck ran over my legs, not my head." Pranthi rubbed her eyes. "I'm careful."

"Do you need anything?"

Pranthi took the plate from the microwave and dumped it in the garbage.

"I'm good," Pranthi said, "really."

***

Coughing woke her up in the night. Pranthi drained the bottle of water she kept beside the bed and tried to get back to sleep. Her brain refused to let her. The mayhem at the zombie walk wasn't at fault. The feel of that woman's kiss had her fevered. She pushed the blanket off, but she couldn't get cool. The woman said she didn't plan for horrible things to happen. Did she lie or did she make a mistake? How did she plan on turning him into a zombie? That was the thing she missed telling the cops: her strange conversation with the woman.

How could she forget that?

Her lungs filled up. The image of those blank white eyes filled her mind and she imagined her chest full of white. Pranthi gasped for air and sat up. It didn't help much. Fortunately, she kept her phone beside her bed.

"Sis," she wheezed into her phone, "I need help." More coughs wracked her body.

"I'll send an ambulance," her sister said.

"Door's unlocked," Pranthi forced her fingers to hit the code on her phone, then fell back on the bed. She made a bet with herself whether the paramedics would arrive before she died. It took all her strength to force air in and out of her lungs. The coughing subsided only because she didn't have the strength anymore. She was drowning in her own bed.

The first she knew that the emergency people had arrived was the cool plastic of a mask blowing oxygen into her. Breathing became a little easier. They slid her onto a stretcher and strapped her down before pushing her out of her apartment. She went back to being afraid of dying instead of wishing she would.

***

The hospital people shoved her into a room with an IV and an oxygen mask. Pranthi half hoped she'd burst into flames from the fever, but decided it was unlikely with the sweat covering her body. People in green came in and took blood. Others put medicine into the IV. Nothing made a difference to the raging thirst. She needed water, but they refused to let her drink anything.

The memory of the man at the park flashed into her mind again. If he felt this thirst, no wonder he went crazy. She bared her teeth and imagined biting someone and drinking them dry. She licked her lips even as her stomach tried to rebel at the idea.

At first the screams in the hall meshed with the screams of the other zombies at the park. Then the crashes of carts and stretchers told her they were here at the hospital. Her thirst and memories merged. Pranthi tried to summon the strength to climb out of her bed. She didn't even have her camera with her. The shouts and screams continued, becoming more frantic.

The door of her room burst open and Kevin shuffled in. His skin flushed bright red and blood trickled from his eyes and mouth. Red covered his t-shirt. He made a low growling sound as he snatched the IV bag and bit into it. Hospital staff poured through the door and tackled him pulling the needle from Pranthi's arm. Blood flowed out onto the white sheets and dripped to the floor. A nurse sidled around the struggle on the floor and put pressure on the arm.

They dragged Kevin away. Then the nurse hooked up the IV on the other arm after putting a bandage over where the first needle had torn a wound.

Pranthi had trouble seeing now. The world looked underexposed, like it had been shot through a dirty filter. She'd had a lens she bought secondhand that took pictures like this. It had been filled with mildew.

A shadow came in and talked about putting in a breathing tube.

"Don't worry," the nurse said, "we'll figure out what virus you have and you'll be just fine. We're just waiting on some tests."

The conversation in the coffee shop floated to the surface of Pranthi's consciousness, like a soap bubble full of white.

"It isn't a virus," Pranthi said just before the bubble burst. "It's a fungus."

Alex McGilvery

HOW CRAZY IS CRAZY?

Constable Dan Pabst knocked on the hospital door and peeked in. Ever since he'd walked in on a sponge bath, he'd been very careful about entering hospital rooms. It didn't help that it was a ninety-year old man getting the bath. Being just finished with his rookie year, he still got the most meaning-less assignments. The full suit, mask and gloves the Center for Disease Control people were making everyone wear didn't add to his confidence.

This room held one Pranthi Chopra who'd photographed the incident at the zombie walk and handed the pictures to the sergeant at the investi-gation. He'd seen the pictures on the front page of the Journal a week ago and didn't want to imagine what it would have been like to have almost died there.

"Come in," a weak voice called from in the room.

Dan walked in with his usual speech prepared, but his mind went blank when he saw Pranthi. He'd been expecting a hardened photographer, this girl barely looked out of her teens. In the tent-like hospital gown she might not even have been twelve. Pranthi sat on the bed with twisted, impossibly thin legs dangling from the side. They were more scar than skin.

"Well, at least you aren't my sister," Pranthi said. Her brown eyes summed him up, slotted him into 'harmless' and dismissed him before he could pull up a chair and sit down.

"I'm here to ask you a few questions," Dan's words puffed against his mask. "I'm Constable Dan Pabst." He waited for the inevitable joke, but she lifted her shoulders slightly. Dan took that as an invitation to continue. "Your photographs have been immensely useful, but I'd like to get some context for them." He opened his notebook and looked at the list of questions he'd printed there to ask her. Lame, she's going to think I'm lame. Dan took a deep breath. It didn't matter if she thought he was stupid, he had a job to do.

"How long have you been shooting zombies?" he asked. The burn of red crawled up his neck as she laughed. Her speaking voice was flat, but that laugh was musical.

"I'm guessing you mean with a camera," Pranthi said. "Though, after this year, I'm thinking of adding a shotgun to my gear bag." She looked up at the ceiling. "This Walk was the fifth I've shot for Kevin. He's the organizer of the events. That's four years. He tried two one year, but the second one didn't go well. People aren't thinking zombie in springtime."

"And you didn't have any trouble at any of the others?"

"If you mean someone chewing the neck of another walker, then no." She coughed, and her whole body shook.

Dan winced in sympathy.

"This walk is a fundraising thing, right?"

"Yeah, the first year it was to bring something for the food bank, but Kevin added prizes and a fee as well as the food. Nobody's getting rich over it, but it is a good event for him."

"Someone said that you arrived in Kevin's car just before the incident."

"My legs got tired," Pranthi said. "They've just never been the same since my mother arranged for a truck to run over my legs. My dear sister swept in to rescue me after the fact. A bit of too little, too late."

Dan stared at her. He couldn't understand the casual way she described the injury to her legs.

"You wear braces to walk?" Back to business.

"Yup, infernal devices of torture," Pranthi said.

"The only thing worse would be living in a wheelchair. If I walk too far, my legs cramp up. If I walk too fast, they cramp up."

"So you stopped to rest."

"No wonder you're a police officer," Pranthi said, her hands kneading her legs. "Yes, I stopped in a coffee shop on the route. Kevin came and picked me up to shoot the winners. I never did get that done. Kevin will be wanting some money back."

"You won't have to worry about that," Dan said then snapped his mouth shut. He sighed and lowered his notebook. "You won't have heard that you weren't the only person infected with this fungus thing. Kevin was one of the ones who didn't make it."

"I think I saw him come into my hospital room."

Pranthi scrubbed at her eyes with her hands.

"Tell anyone I cried, and I'll tell them you fixed a parking ticket for me."

"You drive?" Dan asked.

"No, but my sister does, and she's a menace, never got out of the habits she learned in India."

"Your secret is safe with me," Dan nudged a box of tissues over to her. "The hospital staff say that you told them the infection was fungal, not viral."

"Some crazy woman talked to me at the coffee shop. She ranted about zombie ants and fungus and other stuff," Pranthi's eyes widened. "Suggested I skip the close of the walk." Her already dark skin grew darker and she touched her lips. "She kissed me before she left. Then told me to forget her. All thought of her vanished before I got to the park."

"What did this woman look like?"

"She had these beautiful blue eyes, like the ocean where I was a kid. Blonde hair, might have been real."

"You think she was trying to infect you?"

"Maybe. She never gave me her name, didn't ask for mine. Just mentioned that she made the costume for the guy who would have been the winner if he hadn't gone nuts. His girlfriend too."

"So, she was an ex-girlfriend?"

"More like a wannabe girlfriend," Pranthi said.

"Unfortunately there have been a few incidents, attacks, as well as illness like you had," Dan said. "Your tip about the fungus has saved a lot of lives. Gave the hospital a jump on the tests. We tracked down all the walkers to get them treatment."

"The conversation sort of popped into my head as zombie Kevin was chugging down my IV. Just not soon enough for some," Pranthi wiped her eyes again. "I liked Kevin. He wasn't an asshole. He didn't expect that a photo contract meant he could try to get into my pants. Not that I've had that problem a lot. Most guys run away puking when they see my legs." She looked at Dan as if daring him to say something trite.

"I'm watching your eyes too much to pay much attention to your legs."

"Not bad," Pranthi rolled her eyes. "Though, you may want to make sure the cure is complete before taking me out to dinner. It would be a downer if I went zombie while eating the salad and you had to shoot me in the head."

Dan laughed and Pranthi joined in. She reminded him of his kid sister. Tough as nails on the outside, funny as anyone he'd ever met and soft-hearted when you got to know her.

"I have to ask who you had contact with after the incident."

"Denise and Matt at the Journal. A taxi driver who took me from the Journal to my apartment. Frank, the concierge, the paramedics who brought me in."

"Any physical contact?"

"I don't like being touched." Pranthi closed her eyes for a moment. "We passed around my tablet, I paid the taxi driver. No skin to skin, except for the paramedics bringing me here."

"Here," Dan handed her his card. "If you think of anything else, call me."

She placed the card on the table.

"Be careful with this woman, Dan," she said as if the card put them on first name status. "She checked out all my photos. Maybe she wanted to see if she was in any of them. Then she infected me anyway. This is one out-there nutcase."

"Was she in any of the shots?" Dan lifted his notebook again.

Pranthi shook her head.

"I'll pass that on to my superiors," Dan stood and put his book away. "Thank you for your time."

He stopped and took a deep breath when he got outside the room. Get a grip, constable. She's a witness, not your kid sister. The sergeant will have your badge if you aren't careful.

He consoled himself by planning how he was going to find out about this mystery woman.

He'd underplayed the damage this fungus thing had done. Half the people at the walk had been infected, more than half of those had died. As far at the CDC could tell, anyone who touched the zombie or the girlfriend, or got blood on them. A few of those had gone berserk attacking whoever was closest. Everyone registered for the walk had been called in for treatment. The anti-fungal stopped the cases of illness and the attacks. It might have been worse. The CDC had people like Dan out tracking all contact any of the walkers had with other people.

After he dropped the suit, gloves and mask in the bin, Dan decided the next people he should talk to were zombie man's friends at the university where he'd been an MBA student. He checked his notebook for the name of the man, and chided himself that he hadn't asked half the questions he'd planned. Another time.

The radio news was still all about the zombie fungus as Dan drove from hospital to university. They reminded people of the symptoms and told people to get treatment from their doctor or a walk-in clinic. He hoped the city had enough anti-fungal treatment. They interviewed a zoologist who talked about ants. Too creepy for him, he turned the radio off. Traffic was light so he made good time.

Student services people helped him track down a couple of the zombie's friends.

"Hey, can't help you, man," one said. "Fred bragged about this hot science chick who had it bad for him, but he never dated anyone smarter than him. Never mentioned a name."

At least I have confirmation she exists, sort of.

He talked to a few others, but they all said the same thing in different words. The only difference was the women had more sympathy for the science chick. He thought about going over to the science building to check around, but decided he'd rather be chewed out for missing an opportunity than for letting a suspect know they were after her.

On his way back to the station, Dan stopped at a coffee shop to organize his notes. When he had his thoughts lined up on paper they didn't look as convincing as they had in the hospital, but he tracked down the lead detective anyway.

"Nice work," Detective Leanne Oester said. "Keep it up and you'll be writing your exam in no time. We looked at the tablets on the guy for forensics, but didn't check the files. Thought they were his." She nodded in dismissal, so Dan finished his shift filling out paper work.

ON THE TRAIL OF A MAD SCIENTIST

Detective Oester pulled him out of briefing his next shift.

"I've cleared it with your sergeant," she said. "Grab a coffee and join the task force." She looked at her watch. "We meet in fifteen minutes in squad room A."

Dan walked into the room with his half-finished coffee and almost ducked back out again. He was the only uniform without stripes on his sleeve. Detective Oester saw him and waved him over to where she chatted with the lieutenant.

"Here we are, sir," she said. "Dan here picked up the lead on the woman. Would never have thought to look deeper into the tablets without his information."

"Good job, constable," the lieutenant said. "Take a seat, you think of something, speak up."

"Yes, sir." Dan sat at the back of the room and sealed his lips. The other members of the group settled in and Detective Oester introduced the new information.

"The tablets were wiped," she said. "This woman thought we were smarter than we are. What she couldn't wipe was the record of sale. One was purchased by the victim, Fred Swanther, the other by a Cossette DesLauriers. She is a PhD student in microbiology, specializing in fungi. We learned that she did her undergrad in computer science. We've located her home not far from the university." She waved a paper, "we have a search warrant to go take a look. Some people from the CDC are coming with us. We are going to take control of the house and then let the CDC people do their thing. Once the house is secured, you will do whatever the CDC people say, without question. If there are live samples of the agent she used to infect Swanther, they will need very careful handling. Questions?"

There were a couple of questions, but they didn't answer his question. Would he get to go along? He didn't get the chance to ask. Detective Oester swooped him up and made him ride in her marked car. The Emergency Response Team met them at the corner to the street.

"We've had people watching the place since you called," their squad leader said. "No activity at the house. We had a couple of plain-clothes check the residences on either side. No one is home. We're set."

Detective Oester looked over at the CDC people waiting by their van. They nodded.

"We're a go then," she said. "Sergeant, I want you to feed your sound and mike to me here. I'll watch along with the CDC folks and keep you informed."

One of the CDC people handed out masks and gloves to the ERT officers.

"Wear these. You'd rather be uncomfortable than dead. We think it's transmitted by touch, but I'd rather err on the side of caution." None of the officers argued.

"Dan," Detective Oester said, "I need you to go stop someone for a traffic offense and block the other end of this street. No siren, just lights. We've got this end. We don't want her coming home and getting spooked."

"Sure thing," Dan said. He stuffed his disappointment and drove around the block to find a suitable victim. All they wanted was a uniform to be a diversion. Like kids egging a house and making the youngest keep watch while they had all the fun. Dan breathed deeply and told himself he was being stupid. What else did he expect? To most of those cops he was barely out of diapers. At least he could do what he was told and not screw it up. He parked where he could see the intersection he was supposed to block.

The neighbourhood had seen better days. The trees were huge, but the houses looked run down and most looked like they'd been chopped up for apartments. He didn't think there would be much traffic.

Then a big black truck roared up behind him. Even if it hadn't been playing music loud enough to make his teeth ache, it swerved around him without signaling or even slowing down. He flashed his lights at them and the truck pulled over. He pulled up behind it, carelessly letting his cruiser block the street. He'd get heck if someone complained to the department.

To his surprise the beast was driven by a woman. She rolled her eyes at him and reached for her license and registration before he asked for it. He took the license and registration back to the cruiser and ran the plates as he looked at the driver's license.

"Patch me through to Detective Leanne Oester," he said to dispatch.

"Oester here," she said, "this had better be good."

"The traffic stop you asked me to make," Dan

said, "I stopped DesLauriers."

"So, we're clear at the house," Leanne said. "Good work, delay her as long as you can. There are more units on the way. Don't try to arrest her, we don't know if she's armed."

Dan waited as long as he dared before picking up his ticket book and walking back to the truck.

"You are aware that you ran that stop sign?" he said to her. "And the music was loud enough to make for a public nuisance citation?" He started filling out the ticket, writing slowly and laboriously.

"Look," DesLauriers said, "I'm already late for a class, can't you pick up the–"

The explosion drowned out the rest of her words. He twisted to look at the cloud rising from the streets. How many cops were in the house when it blew?

"Now you've done it," DesLauriers started her truck. Dan tried to reach in to grab the keys, but she slammed the vehicle into gear. He stumbled and fell as she took off. She probably didn't notice the bumps as she drove over his leg.

Two cruisers rounded the corner and started up their lights. She swerved onto a lawn, through a fence and into someone's back yard. The crashes faded away as one cruiser pulled up beside him.

The driver yelled into his radio about an officer

down. Dan didn't pay much attention. Pain invaded his whole consciousness, but even as it did, he imagined Pranthi's eyes as she told him how her mother had had her run over. They looked sad as red agony filled his being and dragged him away.

***

Detective Leanne Oester stood frozen as the rumble of the explosion passed under her feet and dust climbed high into the air. People shouted around her, but all she could do was open and close her hands. She needed to do something, anything.

"Detective," one of the CDC people grabbed her shoulder. "We need to evacuate the area and set up a new perimeter." She handed Leanne a mask.

"What effect might the explosion have on the fungus?" Leanne strapped the mask on.

"Did you see any flame?"

"No," Leanne put her hand on her head to force herself to think. "Strange, a blast that size with no fire."

"The lack of fire is a problem—it means the spores could be live."

"Listen up, people," Leanne shouted. "I know we have people in there, but no one goes near the place until the bomb squad clears it. Put your masks on. I need people on either side of the street. We don't have masks for civilians so get them to use tea towels, shirts, whatever they can find and get the hell out of here. Start on this street. Move fast. Remember the houses on either side of the blast are empty. This is a contaminated zone until we are told otherwise. Use your training."

Her team headed out, most wore the masks that the CDC people gave them. The ones that didn't she'd deal with later. Sirens screamed as they approached from all directions.

"Sergeant," Leanne said, "get on the radio and tell people to create a perimeter, then start clearing houses. We'll start with a circle with a half mile radius." She glanced over at the CDC woman who nodded. Not as certain as Leanne would have liked, but close enough. "Outside that radius, get cars on the streets telling people to stay in their homes."

"Detective," another officer ran up to her. "The suspect fled the scene after the explosion, the constable is down. There are cars in pursuit, but she drove the truck through someone's back yard and we haven't caught up with her."

"Get him to the hospital, call the pursuit off for now, we need feet on the ground here. Get dispatch to put out a BOLO, armed and dangerous."

The bomb squad arrived as they prepared to move back to the perimeter. They had their own masks, but the CDC gave them suits that made the officers look like astronauts as they moved in toward the blast site.

Wind blew the dust to the south across the city, but the heavier particles fell out of the sky and covered the immediate area with grey.

At the perimeter, the captain showed up to take over the scene. He handed Leanne a kerchief. She hadn't realized that she'd been crying until she wiped the mud that was tears and dust from her face. Barring a miracle, four of her colleagues would only come out of that place in body bags.

***

Leanne waited by her car for the bomb squad to clear them to enter DesLauriers' lab. She'd argued with the captain for an hour to get permission to check the lab. The bomb squad took another hour to clear the scene, still dressed in their white suits. The university sent all the students and staff home for the day.

"How much longer, officer?" the university president insisted on waiting with them. Normally, it would have infuriated her, but Leanne welcomed the distraction. She had to focus. She'd worry about falling apart later.

The captain arrived just before the building got the all clear.

"Don't assume that because there are no bombs

that the place is safe," he said. "Be careful."

Leanne nodded and took the CDC woman and another scientist along with her partner.

"You get the video," she said to Detective Hernandez, "I'll get stills." He hoisted the camera in reply.

They clomped down the long hallway wearing white tyvex suits and the masks. Leanne set her mind into crime scene mode to fix the smallest details into her memory.

The floors were terrazzo with a few chips on the edges. Doors had no windows and were covered with cartoons and schedules. Bulletin boards advertised jobs and courses. One board had a plastic bag of condoms pinned to it.

DesLauriers' lab was the final one in the hall. Two windows let light into a space that looked half mad scientist lair and half library. Terrariums sat on tables by the windows. They looked to be half-filled with dirt. Bookshelves lined the other walls. A table held a computer at one end and equipment that she couldn't name at the other. Paper piled up on every free surface.

Hernandez went left, she went right to record the room in as much detail as they could manage. The CDC people hung back until Hernandez passed by the terrariums. The books all had titles that suggested Leanne would fall asleep quickly if she tried to read them. The papers were filled with words that might as well have been in a foreign language.

The terrariums were full of ants.

"Cordyceps," the CDC woman said to her partner. They were pointing at the ants. Something was wrong with them. Strange growths poked out of their backs. They hung unto the highest blades of grass. If one fell, other ants swarmed it and carried it away.

"What's wrong with them?" Leanne asked.

"Fungus," the woman said. "It's my specialty, and why I'm here and not someone else." She pointed through the glass, "Those ants are infected. The rest of the nest will attack them. The fungus changes their behavior."

"Is it dangerous?"

"To the ants," the woman said. "Not to humans, people take it as a supplement." She wandered over to the table. "Do it yourself gene splicing. Heaven only knows what she's been doing here. We'll have to go through all her notes and try to figure it out."

"A witness told us she wanted to turn an ex-boyfriend into a zombie," Leanne said. She forced herself to breathe normally, not to hold her breath or run screaming from the lab. "Could she do that?"

"I hope not," the woman said, "but you can never underestimate the stupidity of some brilliant people. Make sure you and all your people get treatment." She went back to peering through the glass at the ants.

Leanne left with Hernandez to report to the captain.

Alex McGilvery

YOUTH IN FLIGHT

The news reported an explosion in a quiet neighbourhood. One officer was injured by a fleeing suspect, four others were killed in the blast. Oddly, the news said it had been compressed air, not explosives. They talked about how much worse it would have been if it had been C4. People were evacuated for most of the day. Sources claimed that the evacuees were given some kind of treatment before being allowed back into their homes.

The only picture that caught Pranthi's eye was a shot of a woman cop with tears running through grey dust on her face. The kind of shot she wished she could take.

The next week a bombing at a mall in Africa took over the news of the explosion, except for brief coverage of the funeral for the fallen. The entire city ground to a halt while the procession moved through the streets. Pranthi had been sent home by then. She stayed away from the funeral. She'd want to take pictures and it didn't feel respectful.

The news magazine Pranthi wanted to sell her

pictures to decided not to cover the story. The editors wanted real news, not stories about fake zombies, not even fake zombies who tried to eat their girlfriends. It didn't fit with the image of their publication, they told her.

She spent part of the four grand from the Journal on a telephoto zoom lens. After her recent experience, she liked the idea of having a bigger safety zone. The lens gave her an excuse to go out and shoot pictures of the city. Pranthi loved it, even as it tired her hands and arms quicker. Might have to get a light tripod if she was going to use it a lot. She collected a huge array of squirrel and bird pictures, even took some halfway decent shots of peregrine falcons. Dan never called, so they must have wrapped up whatever they needed to do without her.

The weather got colder as the weeks passed. Pranthi broke out her thermals. The metal in her leg braces made it necessary to dress like she lived in the arctic. Her jeans didn't insulate her legs enough by themselves. The new aches from the cold slowed her down, but she refused to stop until she was forced.

As she walked home from a failed attempt to get closer to the falcons, a poster on a hydro pole caught her eye. Skateboarders were to gather in protest of a new bylaw the next day. Time to try some action shots.

She dragged on her layers of clothing and packed her gear bag. The new lens could stay safely at home. As great as the lens was, it added too much weight to the bag if she wasn't going to use it. When she got on the elevator a kid from the next floor up already occupied it holding a skateboard.

"Going to the demonstration?" Pranthi asked.

The kid flipped her the finger.

"Effin' cripple." He dropped his board as the doors opened and rolled out of the elevator doing a little hop over the gap.

Frank yelled at him from his desk, and the kid flipped Frank a bird too.

He jumped down the steps in front of the building in what would have been a great photo op. But only if Pranthi had been lying on the stairs, or even standing with her camera out to catch the look of disgust on the old woman's face. The kid turned sharply to avoid knocking her down and sped away down the street.

"Punk," Frank said as he opened the door for Pranthi.

"That used to be me," Pranthi said.

"Can't imagine that," Frank said as he tried not

to look at her crippled legs.

"Not the skateboard," she said, "the attitude."

Frank shook his head and turned to let the old woman into the building.

Pranthi followed the kid toward the park with the demonstration. The noise beckoned her, but she kept her pace slow. Falling with a couple of thousand dollars in camera equipment didn't appeal to her.

At the park skaters of all ages rode boards, did tricks and worked as hard as they could to upset the mostly older people who held signs suggesting that they do their stuff somewhere else.

She wandered about snapping candids. Skaters jumped into the air as their boards twirled beneath them. Others jumped up to scrape along a concrete wall. She set her camera to take long bursts and let it whir away.

Pranthi took a great series of a group of boarders, one of whom was the rude kid from her apartment, teaching an old man how to skateboard. Kids and old man all laughed hysterically and made it difficult for anyone to stir up real anger over the issue. Even the protesters with the signs cheered when the old guy landed a trick.

Pranthi left when the leaders of the two groups started negotiating access to the park. Resolution of the issues was news, but it made for boring photography.

Pranthi had made it about halfway back to the apartment when something snatched at her camera bag. She grabbed at a signpost to keep from being pulled to the ground by the bag that was strapped tightly to her back. Cold metal bit into her hand.

A riderless skateboard careened into a garbage can while the rude kid from the elevator rolled swearing along the sidewalk. Pranthi let go of the post and walked over to pick up the skateboard. She had to use the board to push herself upright. Heart pounding, she went to the kid who lay on his back still swearing. Pranthi didn't want trouble, and he did live in her building.

"You okay?"

"What do you think?" the kid said when the cursing dried up.

"I could call for an ambulance," she pulled out her phone.

"No!" the kid waved at her. "Mom will kill me if I get brought home by the cops again."

"There are worse things," Pranthi said. She shuffled over to a nearby bench and sat down, still holding the board. The kid made her think about her brother. They'd be about the same age, assuming her brother still lived.

"You hurt, young man?" an elderly woman leaned over to peer at him. "What were you doing?"

"He tried something and fell," Pranthi said. "Just needs to catch his breath."

The kid started laughing, so the old woman walked on. He rolled to his feet with an ease that made Pranthi's hand tighten with envy. He sat down beside her and rubbed his knee.

"Sad day when I'm being fussed over by an old lady and a cripple," he said. "You aren't going to bust me?"

"Why should I? You appear to be working on busting yourself."

"I mean, I tried to grab your sh..." he stopped himself. "Most people would be calling the cops already."

"When I was a child," Pranthi said, "I stole food for my family."

"How did you escape with those..." he pointed at the leg braces.

"They came later," Pranthi said. "I was fastest on my block, no one could catch me. Mother felt begging was more honorable than stealing so..." she shrugged and handed the skateboard back. "You may call me Pranthi. I'm more likely to answer then if you yell 'effing cripple'."

The kid turned a deep red and twisted the board around.

"I'm Jack. Look, I'm sorry, I saw all that gear and just figured it had to be worth a pile of money."

"It is," Pranthi said.

They sat for a while watching people walk past. Her leg braces were always worth a second look, but, sitting with Jack, people watched him and glossed over her. Their looks held suspicion instead of pity. She'd take what she could get.

"You sell the pictures?"

"It is how I make my living."

"You got any pictures of me?"

Pranthi pulled out her tablet and they looked at her pictures. Photo editors didn't enthuse over pictures, as it drove the prices up. Jack's excitement over the shots of him frozen in mid trick was refreshing. She didn't pay attention to the time, so it came as a shock when she shivered so much she feared dropping the tablet.

"Hey," he pulled her to her feet, "take my hoodie. It'll keep you warm." He wrapped it around her and helped her put the camera bag on top. His warmth flowed into her, and eased the ache. "If you think these are cool, I'll get some friends to meet you at the skate park and we'll show you some real moves."

"I'd like that," Pranthi said, relieved that her voice didn't shake from the cold.

"Just leave the hoodie with Frank. He's stuffy, but righteous. I'll get it back okay."

He took off in the opposite direction, pushing his board to crazy speeds and weaving through the crowd on the sidewalk. Pranthi walked back to the apartment.

"That's a different look," Frank said as he opened the door.

"Jack worried I was getting a chill." Pranthi handed Frank her camera bag as she peeled off the sweater. Even inside she wished she had the extra warmth. Time to add a layer or two to her wardrobe.

"There's hope for that kid." Frank folded the hoodie and put it behind the desk for Jack. Pranthi took the elevator up to her room. "I just wish he wouldn't skateboard in the lobby."

One day, the next week, Frank knocked at her door.

"Jack asked me to give you a message," he said. "He even promised to carry his board through the lobby if I delivered it for him right away."

"Thank you," Pranthi said as she took the envelope.

Meet you at sk8 prk. Tomorrow 2. He had

drawn a map so she could find the place.

Pranthi sat down to plan what kit she'd need for the shoot. Her main camera and lenses; she had an older camera that would work for some video. A tripod, and hand warmers. She'd never found gloves that let her work the camera fast enough. It wouldn't fit in her usual gear bag, so she packed it in a wheelie case that she didn't use often. It still had space so she tossed in a blanket.

The taxi driver knew where the park was even without the map. His kid was a skater. When he learned she was shooting there, he texted his son. He dropped Pranthi off and pointed her in the right direction to find the park. The driver waved as he drove off and she walked toward the blaring rock music.

The skate park dominated the side of a hill rising up in three tiers. Stairs and ramps connected the tiers while high ramps and a thing that looked like a clamshell were set around the edges. On one side of the bottom tier was a hole that looked like a waterless swimming pool.

Jack waved to her and she was instantly surrounded by skaters who all had their own idea of what she should shoot and how.

"I will set up in one place to shoot," Pranthi said. "When I have enough there, we will move to the next." She pulled out her camera. "Skate for a bit and let me get a feel for what you do. Then we'll get serious."

The first thing that struck her was the flow of skaters. She'd expected chaos and near collisions, but very few times did someone have to veer off. Once she learned the pattern it became easier to shoot. She started following skaters with her new zoom lens on the tripod.

"We'll start with the stairs," she told Jack when she caught his attention. Skaters lined up to ride the railing down the chosen set of steps or simply to jump down. They encouraged her to come in close, promising not to land anywhere near her. She changed lenses and caught some pictures as close to humans in flight as she'd ever seen. When a skater missed a landing, they'd roll on the concrete cursing before taking their board back from whomever caught it.

At what the skaters called the grind rail, Pranthi learned that skateboarding had its risks. One of Jack's friends had been trying ever more outrageous tricks. Pranthi suspected that his bottle of water was more alcohol than water. He got sloppier as the afternoon progressed. She set up fifteen feet from the end of the rail. Close enough to have mostly sky as background, far enough back that the person designated to protect her from flying skateboards didn't have much to do.

Duckman flew down the ramp and hit the grind on the rail, but when he came off he tried a one eighty. The board snapped when he landed and he went down hard. He didn't roll neatly but landed in a heap. Pranthi feared he'd killed himself, but he came up swearing, picked up on half of his board and threw it against the concrete. It bounced straight at Pranthi. She huddled around her camera and waited for the board to hit. There was the sound of wood on wood and the board flew past on one side of her.

Next thing Jack ran up to Duckman and screamed in his face. She couldn't make out what he said past the curse words. The other skaters didn't say much, but they stood between Pranthi and the altercation.

"Give me your board and I'll do it again," Duckman said, oblivious to the anger that surrounded him.

"Look at your leg," one of the other skaters said. "You busted it good."

"Nah," Duckman said, "I'm good."

Pranthi peered around the people blocking her. Duckman's face dripped sweat, but his eyes didn't look focused. He took a step toward Jack in what was probably supposed to be a threat and went down on the pavement again. White bone stuck through his jeans as blood spread on the cement.

The skaters dragged him off to the side where one called an ambulance while Duckman cursed him out. The rest rinsed the blood off the cement.

"Can't skate where it's wet," Jack said. "Let's try the bowl." He helped her up. "You okay? Some people don't handle that kind of stuff."

"I've seen worse," Pranthi said. Her legs ached at the memory, but she pushed it aside.

She took some photos from the top of the bowl, and set the camera for slow motion video with a wide-angle lens at the bottom. The skaters zoomed past, up the side to do handstands and other tricks Pranthi couldn't name. Not one came close to hitting the tripod in the bowl. Jack fetched her camera, then collected names and emails from all the skaters, even Duckman's, before Pranthi called the taxi to take her home. Just before she climbed into the taxi, Jack put his hat on her head.

"If you're going to be the photographer for the skaters," he said, "you've got to have the look."

As she processed the pictures and chose the best, Pranthi had to push down the envy at the casual way the skaters threw their bodies into the air. She posted a few shots on her blog and Jack put some on his page. Some of the skaters even bought pictures. She managed another couple of visits to the skate park before the first snows came.

The snow made her wish, as it did every year, that she lived somewhere warmer. Her walk was slow at the best of times, in the snow she barely managed to move at all for fear of falling.

So instead of fighting the weather she put away her winter clothes and stayed indoors, walking up and down the hallways to keep her legs from atrophying completely. Jack put some music on her iPod that roared and growled through her ear buds. The anger in it matched her determination. She wore Jack's hat and listened to his music as she forced her legs to drag her up and down the halls.

The other doors in the hall started showing Christmas decorations. Jack asked her one day why she didn't decorate.

"I'm Hindu," she said, "we have Diwali, but it is in a different month each year in the fall. I don't really do Christmas."

Jack shrugged and left it at that.

Just before Christmas, Jack knocked on her door.

"Hi," he said, "I bought you these before I

knew you didn't do Christmas. Is it okay?"

"Gifts are always okay between friends," Pranthi said. She rolled back to let him in.

"It's weird how you don't have anywhere to sit," Jack leaned against the counter.

"Why spend money on chairs I don't need?" she said. "But maybe I should buy some for when a friend comes to visit."

The package from Jack held another hat and a hoodie with what looked like a fur lining.

"You like it?"

"It is wonderful," Pranthi said. "It will keep me warm." She rolled into her office and Jack followed.

"I sold a photo essay to a skate magazine," she said and handed him a copy. The front page was Jack sailing through the air with nothing but clouds in the background.

"No way!" he said. "That's sick." He flipped through the magazine.

"You may keep that copy," Pranthi said. "They sent me a few. I have something else to show you. I do mostly photography, but I've been playing with the video we took." She clicked on a file and a video of the skaters in the bowl came on. She'd cut slow speed and faster speeds and put some pauses in. The background music snarled like the songs he'd given her on the iPod.

"You have to post that," Jack said. "It's amazing." He made her play it half a dozen times. She copied it onto a thumb drive for him and told him he could post it for her.

"Just wait until the summer," he said, "we're going to blow some minds."

Pranthi walked and rolled through January and February. Jack came down to visit after school and on weekends when he wasn't out snowboarding. They made a couple more videos together.

She was shocked to realize she missed him the days he couldn't make it.

ONE LEG SHY OF A COP

Dan pulled the sock over his stump, then attached the prosthetic leg. He hated the thing. It made his stump ache and the difference in weight threw his balance off. He used to run marathons. Now he was lucky to walk a city block before pain made sweat bead on his forehead.

The doctors told him it took some people that way. Their body never got the message that the limb was gone. He had to live with the pain, or in a wheelchair.

He put on his uniform and made sure everything was exact. His girlfriend sighed before hugging him.

"They won't give your job back just because you look good."

"I can't sit around and collect a pension," Dan said. "All that work to get this far, I need just a little more."

"I'll drive you there," Cindy said. She knocked back the last of her coffee and grabbed her keys.

"Don't you have that editing to do? You were

saying the client was getting antsy."

"I work for myself, Dan. I'm giving myself a half day off."

Dan put on his winter coat and negotiated the steps and walk to the car. One foot wanted to carry him to the driver's side. The other was a soulless hunk of steel and plastic. He climbed into the passenger seat and buckled his seat belt.

Cindy dropped him off in front of the station.

"Thanks," she said.

"What for?" Dan extricated himself from the car.

"Don't think I didn't see those white knuckles on the door handle." She waved at him, "Call me when you want me to pick you up."

Dan walked through the plaza. Snow had always been a nuisance, now it was treacherous. He made it to the doors and into the atrium of the station.

"Good morning, constable," Tim, the special officer at the desk, said.

"I would have brought you coffee," Dan said, "but it'd be cold by now."

"I was thinking about sending out a team of sled dogs for you."

"Don't know how to drive sled dogs." Dan

shrugged and opened his coat before he overheated.

"Captain's expecting you," Tim said. "Go on up and he'll be with you in a few minutes."

"Expecting me?" Dan said. He resisted the temptation to put his hands in his pockets to hide the shaking.

"You have been in every day since they let you out of rehab. If you didn't come in, I'd send a car to do a welfare check."

"Thanks, Tim." Dan made his way to the elevators and rode to the seventh floor. The receptionist took his coat and told him to sit.

"You don't need to treat me special," Dan said, then winced.

"It's okay, constable," she said, "I help the mayor with her coat and she isn't half as deserving as you."

Dan sat in the soft chair, trying to keep from slouching. The receptionist brought him coffee and he made himself smile and thank her.

He'd started with his staff sergeant, then the lieutenant, last week he'd worked up the nerve to try to speak to the captain. They'd all been sympathetic, but a constable needed two good legs. Even he had to admit that his prosthetic made him slow.

Dan had been a cop for less than two years. He

didn't feel like quitting.

"The captain will see you now," the receptionist said. Dan looked at the full cup of coffee and shook his head. Walking, he could do, just. Carrying a full cup of somewhat hot coffee was no longer possible. He pushed himself to his feet and walked into the captain's office.

"Good morning, constable," the captain came out and shook his hand. "Glad you could join us. You know Sergeant Connor from the Union?"

Dan nodded and shook the sergeant's hand.

"We like to see people who want to come back to work," Sergeant Connor said. "Every effort needs to be made to accommodate officers returning from an injury."

Dan lowered himself into the chair and allowed a little hope to set his heart racing.

"You have to admit that a return to the front line is not going to happen," the captain said as he sat in a chair facing Dan.

"There are plenty of ways to serve other than the front line," Sergeant Connor said.

"I like working with people," Dan said. "Don't know if I'm cut out for a desk job. There has to be some way that I can still be a cop." To his horror, his voice broke. He had to stop and force himself to breathe. The fear was like the pain; it wasn't going to rule him.

"You see?" Sergeant Connor said. "You can't tell me that you can't use some of his dedication."

"There may be a possibility," the captain said. "I'm waiting on the Chief's approval. More on the community side of things, but you will be working with people."

"He stays a cop; he carries a badge."

"If the chief approves, I believe it will be a fit that will make both of you happy."

Dan listened and watched them. They were fighting over something bigger than just what he would do with the rest of his life. He'd heard the Union didn't like the pensioning off of injured officers. The department wanted able-bodied cops they could shuffle at a moment's notice.

The phone on the desk rang. The captain had to walk over to answer it. Dan put his hands on the arms of his chair to keep them from rubbing his leg.

"Okay," the captain said, "thank you, sir. He's here now. I'll let him know."

He came and sat down again.

"Here's the deal, Dan," he said. "You can talk it out with Sergeant Connor later. I'll send him and you the details. We needed someone in Victim Services. It is mostly a volunteer group, they follow up with emotional support for victims of violent incidents, but there are times when it will be helpful to have someone in uniform be able to respond. We're suggesting you take the training. If you decide it will be a good fit, you will continue in that position. If your rehab brings you to the point where you can pass the physical, you will be able to return to active duty. Even if you can't, or don't wish to, there is a career track available through this posting. You don't need to decide now. Talk to Sergeant Connor, talk to the coordinator of Victim Services."

"When can I start the training?" Dan asked. "I promise I will talk to the Union, but another day sitting around doing nothing will send me over the edge."

Sergeant Connor leaned back in his chair and looked over at Dan. He nodded at the captain who sighed and sat more relaxed.

"I'll walk you over to Victim Services," the captain said. "You will have whatever time you need to make the decision."

Dan pushed himself to his feet.

"Thank you, sir."

He followed the sergeant out of the office. Connor waved and wandered back to his office.

The captain led him to the elevator and down to the main floor. They walked out into the atrium and into an office that wasn't directly connected to the rest of the building.

"I'll let Shelly explain Victim Services to you. Remember that you will remain a sworn officer. It's unusual, but I'm sure you will make it work. What the Chief and I are hoping is you'll be able to concentrate on this zombie thing. Seems to have gone quiet for the winter, but my gut still knots up just thinking about it. You did good work finding DesLauriers." He knocked on a door.

A middle-aged woman answered.

"He agreed?"

"Full pay, sworn officer, the lot."

"Shelly Hadon," she put out her hand and Dan shook it. "I'll give you the tour and we'll go from there."

The captain headed back upstairs.

"Do you know anything about Victim Services?"

"I know I handed out quite a few of your cards."

"Good, that's a start."
***

Dan waved thanks to the cruiser as they pulled out and walked up to the house. Cindy met him at the door.

"Well?"

"I start training tomorrow for a new position,"

Dan said. "I'll tell you all about it when I get this damned leg off."

Cindy brought him coffee and a sandwich, so he sat at the table while he alternated between eating and filling her in on his new work.

"I did some research," Cindy said when he'd finished. "Thought I remembered something from a thesis I edited last year. There is someone at the university who works with the kind of pain you're dealing with. He told me he'd meet with you. No promises, but it's something, isn't it?"

"When?"

"Tomorrow? I told him it was urgent." Cindy's hands tightened around her cup. "I don't want it interfering with your new job–"

"I'll take a break to go and see him," Dan put his hand on hers. "Thanks for not giving up on me. Don't know how I got so lucky."

***

Shelly didn't mind him taking the afternoon to see the doctor at the university.

"Whatever you need," she said. "We'll work the training around your appointments."

He took a cab over to the university and met Cindy there. Dr. Grenfell came out to lead them back to his office. He got Dan to remove his leg and sock before running a series of tests on the stump's sensitivity.

"Well, I have good news and bad news," Dr. Grenfell said when he'd finished. "The bad news is you're stuck with one leg. We can't grow it back. The good news is that we should be able to significantly reduce your pain levels without medication that would impair your ability to function as a police officer." He hooked up a machine to electrodes and placed them on his leg. When he turned it on, the pain rapidly faded away.

"Ah, good," the doctor said. "I'll send you home with a small version of this. There are other things we must do, but I think it likely that you will be able to walk without much pain within a month."

Dan walked out with Cindy. The leg was still a nuisance, but it ceased to be torture.

"I think we should celebrate," he said. "Let's pick up some Chinese food on the way home."

"Sounds good to me," Cindy said, "and I have some other things that don't require two legs." She grinned at Dan and his heart sped up.

"Maybe we should get the food delivered."

THE GODS ABOVE

One Saturday, in March, Jack told Pranthi he was going up on the roof.

"You should come," he said. "It's cool. There are things to block the wind and the sun is warm."

Pranthi put on the fur lined hoodie and took the elevator with him to the top floor. Jack helped her up the stairs to the roof, his arm warm around her waist. She didn't need his help, but didn't mind it either.

In the brief time since he tried to steal her gear, he'd become important to her. Nothing romantic, something more important. Jack didn't ignore her legs, or make her only about them. They were just part of her. As she considered their friendship, Pranthi thought again how Jack might have been the age of her brother if he still lived.

She wasn't going there today. Her brother, whether alive or dead, was a sorrow for a different time. Not something to get between her and whatever Jack was showing her.

The roof was everything that Jack promised.

Most of it was flat with gravel and tar, but boxes and vents stuck out of the roof and people would sit or lay on them and bask in the weak sun.

Pranthi started going up every day. Walking up there meant a view other than the endless procession of apartment doors. A faint whisper in the back of her head sighed with pleasure when she stepped out into the sun.

She stayed away from the edge, though there was a railing surrounding the entire roof. The height didn't bother her if she didn't have to look straight down. Jack loved to stand right by the railing and look down at the people walking in and out of the building.

They were a floor or two higher than the building next door and its roof was also occupied. Pranthi brought up her camera and took pictures of the roof and people. The Journal bought her photo essay and named this new obsession roofing.

All over the city, residents climbed to the roofs of their buildings to take in the sun. Some people weighed in with concerns about safety and others commented about the body's need for vitamin D. One columnist wondered what made the people so interested in populating the roofs of the city, when only a few other places had citizens basking on the rooftops.

Nobody mentioned voices in anyone's heads, so Pranthi kept quiet about the increasingly vocal whispers telling her to climb higher. Clearly, the voice didn't care about her legs.

After a couple of people fell from a building, the city tried to stop people climbing to roofs without proper railings. The roofers went anyway. In most buildings, the management gave up and put up some kind of railing and posted signs telling people they were there at their own risk. That was cheaper than the constant replacing of broken doors.

The TV station called to let Pranthi know they were going to film a story about the roofers from a helicopter and wanted her to shoot pictures from the roof. She passed the good news on to Jack. There would be no problem getting a crowd up there, but she could use a hand lugging her gear up there. She wanted more than just her camera and one lens.

Pranthi just got out of the shower when Jack banged on her door.

"We're heading up," he called through the

door. "You coming?"

"I should get dressed, first," Pranthi said.

"Yeah, good idea. See you there."

Pranthi put on warm clothes, topping it with the hoodie Jack gave her. The leg braces made her ache as soon as she started walking. Pain that reminded her she was alive. Her camera bag thumped onto her back; the reason she still enjoyed living.

Jack waited for her at the stairs and helped her carry her equipment up to the roof. As soon as the door opened, the sound of the helicopter washed over her. Crowds of people gathered and pointed away to the south. Pranthi's heart beat faster. Jack danced with impatience but stayed with her.

Her legs wanted to run and climb to the highest point.

Higher, closer.

Pranthi couldn't remember anything like it since she was a child snatching bread or fruit to run laughing and uncatchable through the crowds. She took a step as if to run and pain ran up her leg into her back. Whatever her legs wanted, the braces kept them trapped. For the first time in years, a tear rolled down her cheek because of what she'd lost.

Climb, run.

All over the roof people pointed at the helicopter and waved. Some shouted and all had broad smiles on their faces. Pranthi pulled up her camera and started taking shots of the celebration. If she couldn't run and climb, she'd photograph the scene.

The chopper hovered near the lower building and the roofers there were also jumping and waving. With her long lens, Pranthi caught the smiles and laughter. The roofers looked jubilant, like they were at a festival, like they heard the same voices Pranthi did.

They crowded under the helicopter, following its motion as it hovered high enough that the downdraft was just a strong breeze. A young man on a roof vent gave a focal point above the mob. He waved and jumped as her camera clicked. Then he fell and disappeared under the roofers. No gap appeared as people stopped to help him.

When the chopper moved away, he lay still on the roof, ignored by the crowd. The helicopter flew toward Pranthi's building and the roofers followed. The railing stopped them, but the push of people in the back crushed the front row against the rail. Their faces should have twisted in pain. They ought to have been screaming for the push to stop. Instead they reached toward the helicopter with the rest.

The railing couldn't take the weight of the crowd. When it pulled up from the roof the mass of people surged forward and over the edge. Falling roofers still smiled and reached for the sky. Even when the pressure was off, people kept going over the edge, as if they would be the ones to defy gravity.

The news chopper flew closer to their building.

Run, climb, jump.

The need in her increased and only the agony of her leg braces kept her grounded. Even so, she tried to run and fell, rolling to protect her camera.

"C'mon," Jack helped her to her feet. "We have to get closer." His face shone with urgency, like Duckman trying to skate with a broken leg—white bone sticking through bloody denim, the image turned her stomach.

"No," Pranthi said. "Something's wrong." All around them people were lifting their hands and faces to the sky. The same, identical expression on each face. Ecstasy captured them, stealing their humanity. Not people at a festival, worshippers.

"What?" Jack said. "The gods are here for us."

He broke for the edge and Pranthi lunged to catch his arm. Jack rolled and kicked to escape her as they fell to the gravel. He screamed something about gods and needing to go to them. He worshipped too. He heard the voice, they all did.

Pranthi couldn't hold him. The crowd surged to the corner waving at the chopper. On this roof, too, young people stood higher on vents only to slip under the uncaring feet of the mob.

Jack climbed a vent, jumping and waving. Pranthi grabbed her camera and caught him high above the crowd. In the frame, he looked close enough to catch hold of the chopper. Tears ran down her face even while she laughed in what might have been joy.

The voice became a roar in her head.

She caught the moment when someone in the chopper saw the havoc from the building behind them. Horror filled the cameraman's face and he turned away from his camera. The chopper lifted and moved away.

The mob followed, crushed against the rail that kept them from whatever ecstatic goal had taken over their minds. Here, too, the railing couldn't hold. No one screamed as they fell. No one screamed when they watched someone fall.

The roar pulled at her and again her legs failed her, dooming her to this grounded existence. Pranthi's numb hands worked the camera as tears streamed down her face. She mopped them away with the sleeve of her hoodie.

Jack jumped off the vent, rolling like he'd missed a trick on his board, then sprinted toward what was left of the crowd on the edge of the building. He leapt up onto the heads and shoulders of the mob and dove out into space.

The sunlight caught him and made him look like a golden bird taking flight. Pranthi prayed that he'd be the one to catch the helicopter, to answer the gods' call.

Gravity pulled him down to pass far below the chopper, arms still spread out like wings. Jack plummeted out of sight. The chopper lifted and vanished into the blue sky.

A knife edge of pain drove into Pranthi's gut as the roar in her head stopped. She fell to the roof huddled around her camera. Her screams blended with the despairing wails of the few people left around her. The ecstasy had abandoned them with the disappearance of the helicopter.

Pranthi didn't care what happened now.

The gods had rejected her.

Only she stopped believing in gods the day the driver of the vegetable truck had carefully crushed her legs beneath the wheels of his truck. He'd collected his payment from her mother while her little brother sat beside Pranthi and held her hand, patting it occasionally as she wept.

Alex McGilvery

THEY WALK AMONG US

Pranthi read the paper spread across her legs in the hospital bed. The Journal put Pranthi's pictures on the front page. Her photos weren't just in the local news, but went across the globe. The first reaction to the story had been compassion and horror. The second had been to blame the news people. Neither the pilot nor the videographer admitted to seeing people falling off the buildings until it was too late to stop it. Who'd expect a helicopter flying overhead to turn rational people into mythical lemmings? Pranthi wouldn't have believed it if the urge to run and jump hadn't invaded her too. What she remembered of Jack's attempt at flight wasn't horror but envy. There, but for a pair of crippled legs, went her.

The third reaction to the disaster was to quarantine the entire city. All the roofers had fungus in their system. The rest of the world didn't want to deal with whatever was going on here.

She threw the newspaper away delighting in the way it scattered through her hospital room. The nurse clucked as she picked up the mess. No extra cookie with supper tonight.

Pranthi pulled out her tablet and researched zombies in nature, but gave up reading the articles after the first couple. She didn't like the idea that something could take over her body and mind. The roofers followed the desire of a fungus which had invaded their systems. Most of the quotes from surviving roofers from her building and the next one involved something about hearing the voice and waiting for the gods. Like Jack said before he died. She resisted the urge to throw her tablet after the newspaper.

Turned out all that treatment didn't kill the fungus, just helped her to survive with it. The woman in the coffee shop had talked about ants and fungus and zombies.

The editor from the Journal cooked up the idea of a special edition on the zombie fungus. Denise wanted her to take the pictures to go with the feature. The research department could deal with the nightmares. Pranthi had enough already. She emailed Denise to turn down the offer.

Tears ran down her face, but the tissues were too far away for her to reach them. She dropped the tablet on her legs and let them come. She'd liked

Jack. He'd been fun to work with on those skate-board shoots. Now he was gone, like her brother was gone, like Pranthi wished she was.

"Knock, knock," a voice from the hall called.

"Come in," Pranthi said. A moment later someone placed a tissue in her hand so she wiped her eyes. Constable Dan stood beside her bed with a strange look on his face.

"I thought you had forgotten me," Pranthi said. The look disappeared and Dan shook his head.

"Didn't forget you," he said. "I followed up on the lead you gave me, which meant a raid on a house. That went completely sideways, killing some officers and leaving me," he thumped his leg, "short a leg. I wanted to stay on, but with only one good leg, I couldn't be front line, so they put me in Victim Services. So here I am."

"I'm a victim, now?"

"Aren't we all?" Dan said. "We're trying to help as many of the survivors of the roofing craze as we find. There have been a lot of suicides among the people who didn't fall from the buildings. Like the people up there wanted to die."

"We were offering ourselves to the gods," Pranthi said. "It doesn't make sense, but that is the best way I can explain it. We were supposed to be up there."

"I've heard that a lot," Dan said. "The roofers weren't a big part of the population, but they tended to be people who were lonely or outsiders."

"Aren't we all?" Pranthi said. Dan left soon after, leaving a card on her table for her to call if she needed to talk more.

***

Pranthi fought with the buggy holding her groceries. The only reason she didn't bring her camera on shopping trips was she feared dropping it in the battle to get her food home. Frank told her to get the groceries delivered, but then she'd never leave her apartment. Every time she went out she'd think about Jack and go back home. For the first time since Pranthi had bought her first camera, the lure of taking pictures wasn't enough to get her past the pain. Strange that emotional pain defeated her, not the agony in her legs.

So she wrestled with the buggy, wishing she had the nerve to curse like Jack at the recalcitrant object. The battle with the groceries kept her from seeing the man until he was almost on top of her.

His eyes fixed on hers while blood dripped from his mouth. Behind him a woman lay in a red puddle on the sidewalk. Like the zombie at the park, this man walked faster than she could, especially with the buggy. She pushed the thing at him. He bumped into it and instead of pushing it out of his way he bounced it forward with each step.

A gap opened in the traffic beside her. Cars rushed up to fill it, but it gave her a chance. Pranthi stepped out onto the road and hobbled as fast as she could manage across the two lanes to the center line. Cars honked at her as they passed, their horns dopplering from high to low. Fingers waved from open windows.

Nothing she hadn't seen before.

Cars flew past on either side, clearing her by inches. Pranthi held her breath and froze. The man untangled himself from the buggy and stepped out on the road. The car that should have hit him switched into the middle lane cutting off the truck beside it. That truck swerved and headed directly at Pranthi.

She stared at the driver who had her hands up in front of her face. Only a few feet from Pranthi, a car coming the other direction hit the truck and sent both vehicles spinning across the road.

The zombie walked through the chaos untouched, as if Pranthi and he were on a deserted street instead of in the midst of mayhem. She was going to die. If the zombie didn't get her, a car would turn her into pulp. If she were braver she'd step into the path of the destruction and be done with it.

The collision spread as brakes squealed and metal crunched. A dozen times she should have been killed, but another car would intervene as if some giant hand played with her life. Horns and people screamed, glass flew through the air drawing blood from her face and arms.

A truck hit a hydro pole and lines dropped across the road and lay like snakes over top of vehicles. The wires sparked and hissed, lighting pools of gasoline. One pool snaked between her and the man. He walked through it becoming a flaming shambling mass.

He reached out to grab her, close enough that the flames heated her skin. She couldn't force her feet to move. To shift even the slightest would be death. To stay frozen was to die.

A car braked hard, the squeal of tires rising over the sounds of chaos. It smacked into the zombie bursting him open, covering the car and Pranthi with red spatters. The car spun into another pole. This one leaned but didn't fall.

There were no more cars. Pranthi's legs quivered like they had been holding her for hours. Even now when the collisions stopped, she stood in the street unable to move. Bystanders rushed to help who they could. Sirens wailed as emergency crews approached from all directions.

Drivers and pedestrians were cut and bruised. People shambled about dazed, like they'd become zombies by the process of disaster. A young woman ran up to Pranthi, but Pranthi refused to move. The paramedics lifted her, still rigid and put her on a stretcher.

When she got to the hospital, Pranthi called Dan. He came over, put on suit, mask and gloves, then held her until she stopped shaking.

"It's starting again," Dan said. "Reports have been coming in across the city."

"Why now?" Pranthi asked.

"Who knows?" Dan said. "There is always some new weird thing. This is just it for this year. We'll figure it out and life will go on."

"Not for everybody," Pranthi said.

"No," Dan said, "but for most people. Humans are resilient creatures."

"What if I become one of them?" Pranthi asked. "I don't want to cause more destruction."

"You were one of the first," Dan said, "and you haven't turned yet. I don't think you're going to. Only a small number of people have." He put a card on the table. "There is a group at the university who are studying the fungus and people who've been affected by it. I'm sure they will want to talk to you. They asked us at Victim Services to try to encourage people to talk to them."

Pranthi picked up the card and looked at it.

"I guess it would be better than hoping I die before I become one of them."

The doctor released her to go home. She agreed that going to the study at the university was a good plan.

Her sister called while Pranthi ate dinner and Pranthi managed not to cry. Just another day of people dying around her.

She sat in front of the television and watched the news report on the crash. Someone had video of her standing in the middle of the road while destruction circled about her. She looked brave in the video, not like she was trying desperately not to wet her pants.

Her sister phoned back.

"You didn't tell me you were in an accident?"

"I wasn't in the accident," Pranthi said, "I was in the middle, not a part of it. Just like most of my life."

"How can I take care of you if you don't tell me

things?"

"Exactly."

"What do you mean?" her sister's voice sharpened and Pranthi held the phone away from her head. The words came out of the receiver garbled now. Pranthi sighed and hung up the phone. Her sister meant well, but could never make up for being a day late to rescue Pranthi. She couldn't explain it to herself, never mind her sister.

Pranthi's body wanted to go to the roof—a remnant of the whispers in her head. She took the elevator up and mounted the stairs, but the doors were chained and locked. Jack might have found a way past them, but Pranthi wasn't going to. The voice wasn't that strong.

For the first time in years, Pranthi took a sleeping pill and lay down on her bed, not caring if she woke or not.

She dreamed that the truck kept missing her legs. No matter how many times the driver tried he couldn't touch Pranthi's legs. Then they put her brother on the road and pushed Pranthi away. The truck drove over him and left just a red spot on the road.

***

Pranthi woke with a gasp. Sunlight beamed in

through her window.

She hadn't been out for weeks. Her camera bag accused her from where it lay on her table. Before she could change her mind, Pranthi picked up her bag and headed out the door.

"Where are you going this morning?" Frank asked as he walked up to open the door for her.

"Somewhere with no traffic," Pranthi said.

"You might try the university, then," Frank said. "My grandson just finished his year there, so there won't be a lot of people. Nice architecture, too, if you like that kind of stuff."

"Thanks," Pranthi said, "a new challenge may be what I need."

She walked out and flagged down a cab. The university campus did look interesting. Gardens surrounded old buildings. She alternated macro shots of early flowers with pictures of the campus buildings. She even found some gargoyles sticking out from the eaves of one of the buildings.

Using the camera again helped the knots in her body to loosen. She was so used to pain that the tightness in her shoulders and back didn't register until it was gone. Instead of making her feel better, it accentuated the pain in her legs. Time to sit down.

Pranthi found a bench in a warm spot and sat, enjoying, for the moment, not doing anything. She rubbed her thighs a little and sighed. Maybe she'd just call a cab to pick her up here. When she pulled out her phone to call, the card Dan gave her fell out.

She was already at the university, why not see what they had to offer? A few seconds later, she had a map of the university on her phone. The research unit was the building she'd found the gargoyles at. Not too far away in a straight line. Before she could change her mind, Pranthi pushed herself to her feet and walked back to the research site.

Just inside the front door a sign directed her to the lab. Fortunately, it was located on the ground floor. Pranthi walked down the hall, passing open doors where people in white coats worked at equipment she didn't recognize. Whiffs of odd smells drifted out the door. As she opened the door to the Fungi Research lab, the scent of fresh coffee wafted through her nose.

"Hello," said a man with a grey ponytail and the ubiquitous white coat. "Can I help you?"

"I would love a coffee and a chair," Pranthi waved at her legs.

The man raised his eyebrows, but pushed an office chair over to her and picked a cup from a pile on the counter.

"This is an odd spot to show up for coffee," the

man said. "What do you take in your coffee?"

"Black is good," Pranthi said. "I was told you were researching the zombie fungus and might want to talk to me."

"Okay," he said, "I'll wheel you into the office we use for interviews."

Pranthi clutched her coffee as he carefully pushed her through a door into a room covered with enlargements of her photos. He picked up a clipboard and sat in a chair by a table in the center of the room.

"Name?"

"Pranthi Chopra."

The clipboard fell to the table as the man stared at her, his face pale and mouth open.

"Gwen!" he shouted just as Pranthi started to worry about him. "She's here. Pranthi just walked in our door."

A young woman burst through a door Pranthi hadn't noticed.

"What?" she said. "You're kidding, right? I thought she was dead."

"No such luck," Pranthi put her coffee down and started to push herself to her feet.

"Please," the man said, "you're the closest we've

come to patient zero. We need your help."

Pranthi sagged back into the chair. The desperation on their faces pinning her in place.

"Okay," she picked up her coffee and sipped at it. "It isn't like I have anything else to do. I'm a photographer. I took most of these pictures," she pointed at the wall.

"I know," Gwen said, "they're amazing. Not just artistically, but scientifically. You can see the movement of the affected people. Do you have more?"

"Hundreds," Pranthi said. "Even more than that. I can bring them in, if it would be helpful."

"Heavens, yes," the man said. "I should introduce myself. I'm Dr. Carter Soriea. I was Cossette's supervisor. We've been trying to figure out what she did, but none of her notes at the university hint at it. Everything at her house was destroyed. If we can duplicate her process, we should be able to treat it more effectively."

"So, what do you want from me, besides my pictures?"

"We've been taking blood samples from people and comparing the amount of the fungus in their system. There appears to be more than one strain, and people react to them very differently."

"Then if you can describe your emotional and

mental state during the incidents that will help us determine how the fungus is affecting your mind."

"Where do you want to start?" Pranthi asked.

***

Gwen and Carter insisted on paying for the cab to take Pranthi home. She didn't protest too much when they insisted on paying her for the rest of her pictures. The check in her pocket was made out in hundreds instead of the thousands that a magazine would have paid, but Pranthi would have given all her photos to them if it helped fight the fungus.

It didn't take long for her to copy all the photos from her drive to a thumb drive. She didn't look at any of them. Let Gwen and Carter deal with that. She packed the drive and her camera to go in the morning.

She spent the day letting them draw blood and helping to arrange pictures on the wall. Some of the time she'd shot bursts. They animated them to study the movement.

"The people on the roof move normally, the man in the park didn't," Carter pointed to the computer screen. "The blood tests confirm there is more than one kind of fungus infecting you, and presumably other parts of the population."

"She only talked about sending people to the rooftops, maybe the zombie thing was a mistake,"

Pranthi swung in the chair and looked at the wall full of pictures.

"It's possible, but Cossette didn't make many mistakes. If she'd simply adapted cordyceps then it could explain the roofers. I have no idea how she managed the zombie fungus."

"Thirst." Pranthi forced her hands to stay on the arms of the chair and not clutch at her throat. "When I was in the hospital, the first time, I remember a raging thirst. Kevin went for the IV bag, not me."

"Interesting. I'll have to give that some thought. There's something else here, too. I don't know if it's another fungus or an immune response. It's weird. I'll send it on to the CDC labs. Whatever it is may explain why you are here drinking coffee instead of tearing out people's throats."

"How come they aren't here, like they are at the hospitals?" Pranthi didn't want to talk about why she survived and people around her died.

"We don't deal with any live culture. They gave us the standards to work with the blood tests and we give them anything new we learn."

***

She'd been going to see Gwen and Carter for almost a week. Time to offer something in return for the small bit of purpose they'd brought to her life.

People who talked to her and had hope of beating the fungus. Pranthi had talked to more people in the months since the Zombie Walk than she had since coming here.

She climbed into the cab and told the driver to take her to the bank; she'd cash the check and treat Gwen and Carter to coffee. She'd bribe the cab driver to carry it in for her. She could buy him one too.

"Wait here," she asked him when she got out.

"Meter's running," the driver said.

"I'll be quick."

Alex McGilvery

EVERYONE DIES SOMEDAY

Pranthi put her camera bag on and walked up the ramp and hit the button to open the door. She liked her bank. One of the old, classically designed banks, it echoed with marble. Security cameras fought with cherubs and fat bankers for space along the ceiling. The teller knew Pranthi and chatted as she went about processing the check without expecting a response.

The first Pranthi knew of the bank robbery was the gun poking over her shoulder and shooting the teller. Red blossomed on the woman's chest as she lay on the carpet on the other side of the counter. Other shots made it through her ringing ears as rough hands pushed her to the floor. No alarm sounded other than the shrieks of the customers. From her viewpoint on the floor, Pranthi watched a man break out through the doors and run onto the street. One of the robbers casually pulled open the door and fired a few shots. Screams came from outside the bank now.

"You are all going to die," one robber said: her voice sent chills down Pranthi's spine. "The only choice you have is whether you die fast, or slow. Piss me off and we will shoot you in the leg and let you bleed to death. Cooperate, and it will be quick. Now pass over your cell phones, tablets and any other tech that you could use to alert the authorities to what we are doing. If you are thinking of calling the police, I will point out that people outside the bank will have done so already. If you want to suffer for redundancy, that's not my problem."

Pranthi threw her cell phone onto the large pile that collected. She pulled off her pack, extricated her tablet and slid it across to the pile too. The robber who did the talking came over and crouched down beside her.

"You're the cripple who takes such nice pictures," the robber said. She lifted her mask to show the woman Pranthi had met in the coffee shop. Her clear blue eyes looked glazed, like no one was home behind them. "Go ahead, get your camera out and take pictures. Maybe your pictures will survive, maybe not."

Other robbers were checking the customers carefully for hidden weapons or tech. They moved in stumbles and jerks. When they pulled off their masks, their faces were blank underneath. None of them spoke, one of them drooled slightly.

One man had slid his cell phone into his sock under his pants. The robbers grabbed it and threw it onto the pile, then shot the man, leaving him screaming in pain on the floor. A woman scrambled to dig her phone out of her purse, but the robber searching her shot her before tossing the entire purse onto the pile.

Blood and gunpowder choked Pranthi's nose, but she put together her camera and started shooting photos of the customers. The man who swore unceasingly as he tried to control the bleeding from his leg. The woman who lay like she was already dead, though blood pumped from the wound in her thigh. There were a couple of children clinging to their mothers with tear streaked faces. Pranthi forced her feelings down and photographed them all. The camera distanced her from her fear. It had always protected her from the world.

She didn't expect to feel fear, but every time her life was threatened her coward's heart thumped painfully and her stomach twisted. Dying must be easier than this terror of death.

Sirens sounded in the distance then wailed to silence as they surrounded the bank. The phone in the bank rang until Pranthi thought her head would explode from the noise. The woman ordered one of her crew to pull the phones from the wall. The bank went silent but for whimpers and curses.

A cop behind a shield brought a field phone to the door and retreated. No one made any move to retrieve it. None of the robbers dug through the drawers for cash, or went into the vault.

Two of them took backpacks off and pulled stuff out of them. Most of what they dropped on the floor looked like bricks of modeling clay. Pranthi had seen enough movies to know it was C4. They put together the bricks and wired them with electrodes. The woman who'd talked to Pranthi picked up a switch and held it in her left hand.

"We're hot, people," she said. "Let's get the payload ready." Two robbers took their packs off carefully and lay them on the floor. They pulled out steel tubes filled with black powder. "Find some stairs, put them on the upper floor. Who knows, something might survive." Two robbers in black shuffled off opening and closing doors until they found the stairs.

Seconds after they mounted the steps, there were screams and shots.

"Oops," the woman said, "forgot about people upstairs. No matter."

Pranthi shot a picture of her. Though her voice

was animated, the only sign of stress was tiny beads of moisture on her forehead. The woman's face was only marginally more expressive than the men who jerked about like giant puppets.

"Do you know the largest living organism on the planet is a fungus? The mycelium of those fungi control forests and plains. That system is as complex as the neurons in our brains. They are the moderating agent that keeps everything in balance. Except for us. The world is dying because of us."

She wandered back and forth more like she was giving a lecture rather than robbing a bank.

"So I gave the fungi a little help..."

"You're nuts, lady," the man with the bleeding leg said. She shrugged and the drooling robber shot him in the other leg.

"We are a stain on this planet," the woman continued like she'd never been interrupted. She walked over to the window and peered out. "My, my," she said, "everyone is here." She scratched at her arm and white powder drifted away.

"You're infected too," Pranthi said. She cringed waiting for the bang of the shot and the spike of pain, but the woman laughed.

"We all are, but I was first. I lay in the woods and listened. I breathed in the forest air and knew what I had to do. Humans had to go, they were breaking up beings that had existed for millennia. The fungus told me what I had to do. It wasn't hard. The Zombie Walk was a test. If they hadn't clued in that the infectious agent was a fungus, there would have been no stopping it. Their treatments weakened the link."

"So, now what?" someone asked. The woman pointed to the young man and crooked her finger. Two robbers picked him up and dragged him to the door.

"You run," the woman said. "If you make it, you're free." One robber pulled the door open and the other pushed the young man out the door. He vanished from Pranthi's sight as he bolted for the street. The two robbers fired a few shots and let the door close. They didn't laugh or smile. Their faces might have been carved from plaster.

"Suggestion," Pranthi thought out loud. "The fungus works by suggestion."

"Aren't you the bright one?" the woman said. "The fungus weakens the higher brain functions leaving the person pliable and easy to control. How else could it get all those people to climb to the roof? Then it waits for the right stimulus to come along to finish the job. Makes it easier for me to recruit helpers, though they don't last long."

"The gods," Pranthi said.

"Our need to believe in something bigger than us, or to rationalize what we're already doing. The world provides more than enough suggestion to supplement the fungi's need to get high up."

The woman got up and walked around the bank peering out of windows.

"Come on, come on," she said, "what are you waiting for?" She picked another person at random and sent them out the door to their death.

"We need to try something else," the woman said, "they aren't taking the bait."

"Uuurgh," the drooling robber said and dropped his gun. He picked up a woman from the floor and started gnawing on her neck. Red covered both of them. The DesLauriers shot the robber in the head, then left the woman to gurgle on the floor.

"Anyone else planning to go zombie?" she asked her crew. One of them raised a hand and she shot him too.

She peered out the window.

"Well, finally," she said and pointed to one of the children. "Let's go, sweetheart."

"Take me instead," Pranthi said. "Shooting a cripple will create as much fuss as a kid, and my legs are hurting." She packed her camera away and pushed herself to her feet. The gear bag went on her back as she limped toward the door.

The woman shrugged as the boy's mother clutched him to her.

"Fine then, let's get this done," she waved Pranthi out the door.

Police and emergency vehicles lined the street, people crowded in behind them. Officers pointed guns at them. A cop shouting in a megaphone broke the silence.

"Give yourself up! You can't escape."

"So predictable, make it look good for me."

"You want them here for some reason," Pranthi said. "This isn't about robbing the bank."

"Smart girl," the woman said. "If all the police are here, they can't be somewhere else. A little birdie told me Gwen and Carter found patient zero and were actually making progress on a cure. Can't have that."

The woman pushed Pranthi away. The only way she could stay upright was to hop a few steps forward. She managed to make the first step. Then the woman shot Pranthi, hitting the six thousand dollars-worth of camera gear in her backpack. The sounds of shattering glass cut into her soul. Pranthi rolled down the steps to the pavement and tried to look dead. Three more shots hit her back. Burning pain through her body told Pranthi at least one bullet made it past the camera.

The woman laughed loudly. Then there was the crack of another shot from further away. The woman grunted and fell. Sudden weight on Pranthi told her the woman had fallen on her.

The tiny cylinder bounced away. Pranthi tried to make her hand move to grab it, but her arm refused. The little cylinder clicked and popped open.

ONE-LEGGED COP

Dan walked out of the clinic on the university campus. After months of work, he could move almost normally with his prosthetic leg. Still a long way from passing his physical to get back on the front line, but he no longer felt knives stab into the stump at every step.

Each time he left here, he reminded himself he had Cindy to thank for this relatively pain free existence.

His cell phone buzzed an hour before his next appointment. Another survivor of the roofing craze that killed hundreds through the spring and left many more suicidal. Pranthi's building wasn't the only one, but it was the worst. Dan was no psychologist, but some people took comfort in having a uniformed officer listen to their struggles. If it helped people, he wasn't about to stop.

Since he had some time, Dan decided to stop by the research lab and get the latest. Maybe they'd have something for his client to make him feel less invaded. It would be as fast to walk across the quad as it would to drive and try to find a new parking spot. He'd found it while taking a test walk for Dr. Grenfell after a session with the electrodes.

A black van parked illegally in front of the clinic. Old habits made Dan phone dispatch to run the plates.

"Plates return as stolen," dispatch said. "Reported last night. Stand by for back up."

"Ten four," Dan said and found a spot to watch the van where he wouldn't be noticed by people coming out of the building.

"Stand by on the back up," dispatch said, "an armed robbery and hostage situation has taken up available units. We are directing a unit from an outlying station. ETA is 30 minutes."

"30 minutes," Dan slumped against the tree. He considered calling his next appointment to cancel, but he'd need to hang up to do that. It'd be tight, but if he left as soon as back up arrived, he'd make it.

Shots came from inside the building. A high-pitched scream chopped off after another shot.

"Shots fired," Dan shouted into his phone.

"Copy that," dispatch responded. "Hold fast, back up ETA 15 minutes."

Dan reached to where his gun should have

been on his belt. He wasn't on active duty. He carried a badge, but no gun. Who would think that a Victim's Services officer would need a gun?

Movement behind the building looked like people running from a side door. Dan willed them to run faster. No more shots came, none of the people stumbled. Some yelled into cell phones. Good, the responding officers would have more information.

His palms sweated and his good leg quivered in readiness to run into the building. He had no idea how many people were in there or even where in the building they were. Going inside was a horrifically stupid idea.

Only a white knuckled grip on the bark of the tree he stood beside kept him from humping his way across the street and into the research lab. His heart pounded thunderously in his ears.

The wail of sirens came closer. A piece of bark came off in his hand and crumbled. Three men ran out of the building. Two climbed into the van, but one shambled and weaved like he was drunk. A shot from the van and the drunk stumbled. Two more shots and he lay still on the sidewalk.

A police cruiser skidded around the corner and blocked the van's escape route. The officer jumped out and pointed his gun across the hood of his car.

The van swung in a half circle only to be blocked by a second cruiser. The driver of the second cruiser had his gun pulled but he hadn't parked at an angle across the road so he didn't have the bulk of the car to protect him.

A hail of shots came from the van. The officer returned fire, but was hit. He fell to the pavement, hand against his shoulder. Red poured over his hand turning the blue uniform black.

Dan didn't know he was running until bullets buzzed past him. The van roared toward him, but he managed to get across to the fallen officer, grabbing him with one hand and pulling him away from the speeding vehicle.

The weight spun Dan around so he could see the barrel of the gun held by the passenger of the van track him. The muzzle flashed twice before the van passed.

The first shot hit Dan's vest and made him curse, the second blew the driver's brains across what was left of the side window. The van swerved to the right and hit a tree. Passenger and driver flew through the windshield. The driver smacked into the tree, but the passenger sailed clear. Somehow he still had his gun in his hand and turned to shoot at Dan.

The bleeding cop shoved a gun into Dan's hand as the passenger started shooting. Bullets hit the cruiser behind them as Dan lined up the gun and put three bullets in the center of mass. The shooter fell to his knees but lifted the gun again.

Dan's last shot hit him between the eyes and the man dropped face first on the road.

The other cop came running. She kicked the gun away from the man on the road, then came over to check on Dan and the other cop.

"Medics are on their way," she said as she put pressure on the bleeding cop's wound. Dan went to the cruiser and popped the trunk to get the first aid kit.

"You should be sitting down," the woman officer said. "Even if you didn't feel it, I saw you get hit at least once in the leg and once on the vest."

"Yeah," Dan pulled out a field dressing and handed it to her. "I'll have a bruise in the morning."

"People bleed out from leg wounds," she said.

Dan looked down at his legs. There were two bullet holes through his pant leg. He started laughing, and thumped his leg.

"Fake leg," he said, "I'm glad they didn't shoot the good one."

They huddled by the car until the ambulance

arrived. The medics lifted the injured cop onto a stretcher and were away again. More cruisers arrived.

"We need to check the building for victims," the sergeant said and started detailing who would go where.

"Wait," Dan said.

The sergeant wasn't someone he knew.

"Constable," the sergeant said, "there may be people in there in need of assistance."

"There may also be bombs," Dan said. "It's likely enough that the same woman is involved in this as in the explosion that killed four cops last winter."

"Stand by," the sergeant said and called dispatch. "Okay, we have a problem. The bomb squad is at an active scene. The backup crew is being called up, but it will take at least an hour before they get here. I don't want to wait an hour to check the building."

"There were people leaving a side door," Dan pointed to the side of the building. "If we're going in, that's probably our safest bet."

"Who put you in charge?"

"I know the layout of the building," Dan said, "at least the main floor." He pulled out his notebook and sketched a layout for the sergeant. "The door they left through is from a stairwell. We get access to everything but the main floor by that stairwell. The main floor is the problem. I think they were after the research lab. If there is a bomb, it will be there. We can clear everything but that easily enough. From what I heard, there won't be any survivors in the lab."

"We do it the constable's way," the sergeant said. "No one tries to access the main floor. We check the rest of the building. Carefully, people. Just because junior here thinks they stayed to the main level, doesn't mean they didn't leave any surprises anywhere else. It will ruin my day if I get blown up." He pointed at Dan, "You will stay here and keep people clear. Brief the bomb squad when they arrive. You," he said to the woman officer, "go around the building, make sure there are no civilians in the vicinity. Then you'll take station at the back of the place."

He led the remaining officers into the building.

Alex McGilvery

THE GODS BELOW

The explosion stomped on her and forced all the air from her lungs. The world went from bright and sunny to gloomy in an instant. She could see things flying away from her, people, cars, trees, bits of building, even chunks of road. The force stretched her like she had been transformed into modeling clay and hands pulled on either end of her.

Then the shockwave passed and air returned. It hammered her into the pavement and crushed her breath again. Pranthi partially expected to be crushed by pieces of the bank returning to earth, but all that fell was dust.

The dust fell endlessly, coating Pranthi in a grey blanket and making her choke and sneeze. She struggled to get an arm to her face so she could breathe through the fabric of her sleeve. Each breath had to be deliberate. Her body wanted to stop, the weight of the woman's corpse on her back wanted her to stop, the dust wanted her to stop. Pranthi pulled in air through her sleeve until the fabric clogged, then found another spot on her sleeve.

"Breathe, Pranthi," her brother said. He crouched beside her. "It will all be over soon. The pain will stop."

He was young, like he'd been the last time she saw him. Too young to understand the agony of twisted and shattered legs. Her mother wanted to have his legs destroyed to make him a better beggar. Pranthi argued and argued, until finally she offered her own legs in his place.

Then her sister rescued her and doomed her brother anyway, but too late for Pranthi. What good were crippled legs if they didn't save her brother? After all these years, she didn't even know if he was still alive.

Her mother and brother had vanished after Pranthi's rescue. Her sister tried to get relatives to find them, but they said they knew nothing. They sent money to a bank, but all they knew was that someone collected it.

"It's okay, Pranthi." Fungi grew on her brother's legs, all over his body. He patted her hand as bits of him fell off until all that remained of him was scattered mushrooms like she'd buy in the grocery store.

Her stomach rebelled and tried to vomit, but she couldn't get her face clear. She choked and coughed in the dust. Red spots clouded her vision.

"We've got a live one!'" a voice shouted above her. A hand cleared the mess in front of her face and put a mask on her. The weight vanished from her back and she screamed as pain returned.

Hands picked her up and placed her on a stretcher. They carried her through a wasteland of grey destruction. Hands and faces poked up through the dust, stained with black. Cars lay on their sides and backs. Stumps of twisted wood clawed their way up. They slid her into the back of an ambulance and a new mask was placed on her face.

Pranthi closed her eyes as the ambulance moved away.

"Is she the only one?" a voice asked.

"So far," another voice answered.

***

After they heard about the explosion on the other side of the city, they evacuated the university and closed off as much area as they could manage.

Several hours later, the bomb squad had disarmed the bomb under the table in the lab. Detective Oester grabbed Dan and made him walk through the scene with her and Hernandez.

"I wouldn't normally put you through this," she put a hand on his shoulder, "but you've been in here and maybe can tell us if anything is missing."

Dan nodded and followed her into the building. A body lay in the hall. The white coat now mostly red. He told himself to breathe slowly.

"Bomb squad found a few people hiding in the labs, but most were empty. That guy was unlucky. Shot in the chest means he probably surprised the gunmen. The rest hid, smartest thing they could have done." They reached the lab at the end of the hall.

"Bomb under the table, trip wire across the door. Looks like a cell phone as a remote trigger. They planned to blow the place when they were clear."

A body with red hair lay face down in the corner, blood staining her coat.

"That's Gwen," Dan said, "I never did find out her last name. She was Dr. Carter Soriea's research assistant." He walked around the room. "Nothing else here looks out of place. They met with survivors through there." He pointed to the door then followed the detectives through into the lab. Dr. Soriea lay against the wall buried by the torn up photographs that had covered the walls.

"All those pictures, or most of them anyway, were taken by Pranthi Chopra, a talented photographer who kept being in the right place to take pictures of the zombies. She'd just come in to work with Dr. Soriea and Gwen the last week."

"Might be the trigger," Hernandez said. "Maybe this Chopra is special."

"Dr. Soriea told me that she was the closest to patient zero they were going to get. Her blood told them a lot about the fungus they were dealing with, maybe even hinted at a cure."

"Better track her down," Detective Oester said. "The CDC will want to talk to her. With DesLauriers out of the picture, she'll be the best chance to get ahead of this thing."

"I'll call her," Dan said. "I've got her number from meeting with her after that crash."

Oester nodded and pushed open the door to the next room. Glass and blood covered the floor. Files lay strewn about and several filing cabinets gaped open. Computers were gutted and the monitors smashed.

"I don't think we'll learn anything more from looking at this mess," Detective Oester said. "Thanks for your help, Dan."

Dan left the building. He stopped on the pavement to breathe until the urge to be sick vanished. He'd seen bodies before, but not people he knew. He'd track Pranthi down tomorrow. Right now he wanted nothing more than to get home to Cindy.

***

Cindy ran out of their house and threw herself at him, clutching him tight.

"Ow," Dan said, "not so hard."

She dragged him into the house and watched as he changed from his uniform into civilian clothes.

"I heard about the bomb," she said, "I was so worried about you. You're Victim Services, you wouldn't be at a bank robbery, but I kept imagining you lying dead on the street. What happened?" Cindy touched the bruise on his ribs.

"Oh, yeah," Dan said, "that's where I was shot. Good thing I was wearing my vest."

"What do you mean 'oh, yeah'? How do you forget that you were shot? You didn't tell me about that."

"It's been that kind of day."

***

Pranthi climbed out of bed and used the crutches to hobble to the bathroom. Too much trouble to put the leg braces on for the couple of steps. Voices in the hall held tinny conversations. The explosion damaged her hearing, so everything distorted almost beyond understanding. Ironically, the woman's body on hers was the only reason Pranthi survived.

Endless lines of investigators asked the same questions. Pranthi gave the same answers. She didn't know why the woman had done it. Maybe it was the fungus, maybe she was insane before the fungus invaded her system. They stopped coming, stopped asking, took her ruined camera gear away and left her alone.

Dan came and listened as she told the story her way. There were dark circles under his eyes and he carried his gun again. He didn't say much, only asked her to contact the Center for Disease Control.

"The hospital already did that," she said. "I got breaks from trying to answer questions while they took blood and other samples from me. They told me I was lucky to still be alive, so I threw them out of my room."

Pranthi's sister came and left when Pranthi cursed her for rescuing her instead of her brother.

"Your brother didn't want to leave," her sister said the next day. "I tried."

"He was a child," Pranthi said. "You could have taken him."

"I could only take one," her sister said, "I chose to take you."

Pranthi rolled over to put her back to her sister

who left without saying goodbye.

After a couple of days alone in her hospital room, Pranthi got up and dressed, then put her leg braces on and walked out of the hospital.

A cab took her home through the dust and grit that covered the city.

Frank wasn't there, so she wrestled with the door to get in. The battle left her exhausted, but she refused to stop until she sat in her wheelchair in her apartment.

She lived on water and ice cream until she could get a grocery store to deliver some food.

Pranthi wheeled about her apartment at a loss for what she should do next. She looked at camera gear on Ebay, but nothing interested her.

She ended up watching the video she made with Jack over and over while she cried endless tears.

Days dragged into weeks.

She checked out the news.

Zombies and roofers were showing up around the world. Speculation was the bank blast had been powerful enough to push spores up into the jet stream. Others talked about packages of spores being sent through the mail. No one knew anything for sure.

As in her city, the numbers of people affected weren't large, but they were enough to be disruptive.

People in the tropics cooked in the sun waiting for the gods. Food production slowed and pundits feared starvation would claim millions.

Riots and looting became common; violence broke out as countries tried to close their borders to the threat on the ground while they breathed contaminated air. Masks guaranteed to filter out the spores were popping up across the globe, too late to make any difference.

Something new appeared. Mobs of people attacked others and tore them apart. The rampaging hordes were uncontrollable. One infected person could set off a riot that left entire blocks burning. Cities, and even countries, fell out of communication.

Pranthi turned off the news and went back to crying over Jack's video.

***

Her sister came to the apartment a couple of months after the hospital visit. Pranthi put on water for tea. She never had bought a chair so her sister stood while they waited for the kettle to boil.

"I worried about you."

"I'm surprised you still care after the way I treated you at the hospital."

"It will take more than that to chase me away,

but I thought I'd give you some space."

"Thanks."

"Maybe it's time to talk about our mother. I didn't want to, because I wanted to protect you, but I think I was more protecting myself." She perched on the edge of the table while Pranthi made tea. "Our mother sold me as a bride to a man in Delhi. I was lucky and he wasn't a horrible man. Much older than me and old fashioned, but I think his mother pitied me. We moved here when my husband opened an office for his export business. I think it was a disappointment to him we never had children, but it meant he was willing to accept you coming to live with us."

Pranthi poured the tea and lifted her cup. She rolled it in her hands but didn't drink.

"I'd heard from relatives and friends that Mother was getting unstable, but you were already in the hospital by the time I got there. She was furious that I wanted to take you away. In the end, I bought you, the same way my husband bought me."

"So that money I sent to her..." Pranthi put the cup down and sloshed tea across the table.

"Was the gift of a loving daughter and sister. I made a one-time payment which caused the only serious fight my husband and I ever had."

"There's no hope for brother?"

"I don't know. I'm trying to find a way to go and look for him myself, but I need to know you will be okay before I go."

"I don't know if I'll ever be okay again." Pranthi started shaking.

Her sister came around and hugged her and dried her tears.

"I can wait, if you need me too."

"No, I need you to find him, tell him I love him."

***

Pranthi stayed in her wheelchair to see her sister out of the building. When the elevator opened, a new concierge came over to her.

"You must be Pranthi. Frank told me to take extra care of you. He's gone to his son's home to take care of the kids."

Pranthi didn't ask why Frank would need to take care of his grandkids, she didn't want to know. She missed him but was glad he was safe.

Her sister bent down and kissed Pranthi on the

cheek.

"I do love you, Pranthi."

"I know, I love you too."

Her sister started toward the door when Pranthi rolled forward and grabbed her arm.

"Wait, that man out there isn't right."

"I'll phone the police," the concierge said. After speaking briefly on the phone, he pulled a shotgun out from behind the desk. "Stand over here, out of sight, they don't get as agitated if they can't see you." The doors locked with a clank.

The zombie stumbled against the door and left a smear across the glass. He pounded on the door until his broken hand left bloody streaks behind.

Finally a police van pulled up, and two officers in white suits and masks climbed out. They split to approach the man from either side, carrying shotguns. When the zombie lurched toward one officer, he fired the shotgun, trapping the zombie in a net. The other officer ran to the van and grabbed what looked like a tarp. They wrapped the zombie up and put him in the back of the van, then poured a liquid which bubbled on the concrete steps over the blood. The window they sprayed with something which turned the blood black before sliding to the ground.

"I'll let you out the side door," the concierge

pointed the way. Pranthi gulped, then touched her sister's hand briefly before returning to her apartment and watching endless repetitions of the video. She imagined her brother flying on a skateboard like Jack had.

* * *

Dan showed up at the station in uniform with his gun. He'd gone back to driving a squad car and being a cop. They were so short of people that even a one-legged man could be a cop.

Nobody quite knew what that meant now.

In other cities, mobs raged out of control after tearing apart an infected human. Here they didn't have that problem, they were all infected.

He'd had to shoot a few zombies who shuffled bloody-mouthed after the living. Those were the easy ones, though they had special patrols to control the shamblers without needing to shoot them and spread their blood about.

When looters at a store pulled a gun on him, he'd shot all three. By the end of his shift, the brass cleared him for duty the next day. No one asked any questions.

The mayor wanted a tough message sent. They would remain civilized until the scientists found the cure.

Dan wasn't sure what was left to save. He'd try

though.

He'd try.

The only good thing was Cindy worked from home, connecting with her clients over the internet. He double checked the lock every day before going to work and called her whenever he had a chance.

They both needed to know the other was alive.

Cindy told him the news reports were hinting at a cure. Something about blood samples sent to the CDC before the bank explosion and the murders at the university. It might not be possible to cure it completely, but with encouragement the fungus could be made more benign.

Benign would be good.

He climbed into his car and headed out to patrol the streets.

The everyday bustle of people on the streets was a surreal counterpoint to his task—spot and isolate anyone who looked like they'd gone zombie. Stopping looters and dealing with other crimes came a distant second-floor.

"Report of a zombie at Washington and 4th."

"Ten four," Dan said. "Car 410 in the area. I'll check it out."

"Remember your training."

"Copy that."

Dan pulled onto Washington and saw the old

man stumbling down the sidewalk. The overfilled grocery cart acted as a walker. He parked and got out of the squad car. The zombie gear could stay in the trunk for this one.

"Clear on the zombie," Dan said into his radio as he headed over to talk to the poor guy. Had to be the third time he'd been called to this 'zombie'. Didn't help that the old guy hated cops.

Dan struggled to remember the man's name. Yuri, that was it. He'd brought his family over after the Soviet fell apart. Then his family had fallen apart, then his health.

Yuri looked up and mouthed words at Dan. Moving quicker than Dan expected, he pushed his cart onto the street. A wheel caught in a drainage grate and it tipped. Dan moved faster. He wanted to get Yuri and his stuff off the road. Yuri looked despairingly at his cart, then headed across the street.

An engine roared as a red truck outfitted with a chrome brush guard accelerated. Yuri didn't even have time to look up before tons of steel spread him in a bloody mess across the street.

"Yehaa!" a cry of triumph came from the truck as it pulled over. "Did you get that? We're real zombie killers." The driver and passengers continued to high five each other and shout expletive laced congratulations at each other until Dan pointed his gun into the truck.

"Out of the truck." He'd never worked so hard not to shoot someone before.

"What? We just nailed that zombie for you. You should be giving us a medal."

"Yuri was no zombie, just an old man with Parkinson's. You aren't zombie killers, just garden variety murderers."

The man with the camera turned away from Dan's gun and vomited on the driver. They began screaming at each other as Dan called in for a cleanup crew.

***

After her sister left, the whispers came back to Pranthi, at first an inarticulate urge. She'd zone out watching the video and come to facing south, away from the computer. Moving the desk was too much work, so she got used to swiveling back to face the screen.

Then one day she found herself staring out the southernmost window at the end of her hall. A line of green in the distance called to her, but she wheeled back to her apartment and tried to continue living as she had been. Normally, by this time, Kevin would be contacting her to shoot the Zombie Walk. There'd be no walk this year, only zombies.

Pranthi never wanted to photograph another zombie.

The whisper wouldn't leave her alone. Pranthi woke lying across her bed, facing south with tears in her eyes. That day she heard words.

Come to us.

The walls of the apartment closed in on her as the whisper grew stronger. Pranthi sent a message to her sister. *I'm sorry. I hope you find our brother. I love you.* Then she transferred all the money in her bank, except for a couple of hundred dollars, into the account which her mother should have access to. She put her leg braces on and left her apartment with a picture of Jack glowing on her computer. She didn't bother to close the door behind her.

The tug in her heart pulled her south, as the sight of the helicopter had pulled her up.

She rode down in the elevator facing the south wall.

The new concierge came over.

"Can I call a cab for you?" he asked.

"No, I think I'll walk for a while."

Pranthi walked out through the door the man

held for her and headed south.

People crowded the streets. They carried bags of groceries or walked dogs. Some kids skateboarded past shouting at people. Strangely normal for the end of the world. Maybe it wouldn't end. The headlines on the newspapers intermingled talk of a cure with reports of disaster.

When she got tired, Pranthi hailed a cab.

"Go south," she said. The driver shrugged and drove south.

"Look, lady," he said after a bit, "the only thing south of here is the state park."

"That will do," Pranthi said.

He pulled up in a deserted parking lot.

"Here you are," he said. "How are you going to get home?"

"I have my cell phone," she said, "I'll call you when I'm ready to go home."

Almost here.

The path led cool and inviting into the forest. Pranthi didn't know why she hadn't come here before. No dust clogged the air or left grit under her clothes to chafe. She found a stick to help her walk and followed the path, following the tug in her heart whenever it split or met another path.

Off to her right, a patch of golden light beckoned. Pranthi stepped off the path and headed toward it. Fungi in a rainbow of colours surrounded her. They grew on trees and fallen logs. Mushrooms pushed out of the black earth in reds and whites and taupes. What color fungus took over the ants? What color fungus lives in my body?

The golden light turned out to be a tiny clearing in the forest made by a fallen tree. Its roots towered over her head, black dirt lay open to the sky with only drifted leaves and a few white fungi pushing out into the sun.

Pranthi dropped her stick, then took off her leg braces and threw them away into the trees. Her shirt came off easily. Her pants were a struggle, but they, too, went into the brush that surrounded her.

She lay on the dark ground by the roots of the fallen tree. The sun warmed her skin while the cool, damp earth caressed her back. She imagined white filaments growing out of her skin into the ground, anchoring her in place. Following them with her mind she closed her eyes and stopped thinking about her body, her breathing, even her heartbeat became unnecessary.

The trees around her reached up to the sky and deep into the earth. All through the soil filaments ran like nerves carrying her awareness into the woods. Flowers, grass, trees, fungi, even the animals connected to the network.

They covered the surface of the globe, whirling at unimaginable speed, then gradually slowing down to the speed of the forest.

The rustle of leaves became almost words speaking just to her.

Join us.

Her last breath puffed out a cloud of spores to dance on the breeze. Some fell to the ground to join the filaments already spread through the soil, but others wafted into the air to drift to seed other places and other people.

Alex McGilvery

ACKNOWLEDGMENTS

Every book is a team effort, even if the contribution is giving space for the crazy author to write instead of vacuuming. So huge thanks to my wife and muse, who'll never read the book because she doesn't like zombies.

Every book needs some critical eyes on it so the input of Gary Buettner and Rebecca Charlton is much appreciated, especially for making all the characters important. The folks at Critique Circle also deserve a tip of the hat as they waded through an early version and gave great suggestions.

Finally, a thank you to my proofreader Serena Antal, who worked hard to find all the places where my fingers couldn't keep up with my brain.

OTHER BOOKS BY ALEX

The Regent's Reign
Calliope and the Sea Serpent
Wendigo Whispers
The Gods Above
The Heronmaster
Blood and Sparkles and other stories
Princess of Boring
By the Book
Sarcasm is My Superpower
Tales of Light and Dark
Like Mushrooms (poetry and photography)
Playing on Yggdrasil
The Unenchanted Princess

Alex also has stories in:

Song of the Axe
Canadian Creatures
Words on the Rocks
Beyond the Wail
Collidor Stream Collection 2016